The Devil Wears Red

Book Three of the Tewkesbury Chronicles

By

Jo Gillespie

The Devil Wears Red
Book Three of the Tewkesbury Chronicles

Copyright © 2017 by Jo Gillespie

Published by A Page in Time

Printed in the United States of America

Cover Design by Indie Desingz

http://www.indiedesignz.com

Proofreading and editing by Rita M. Reali, The Persnickity Proofreader

ISBN-13:978-0692924587

ISBN-10:069=2924582

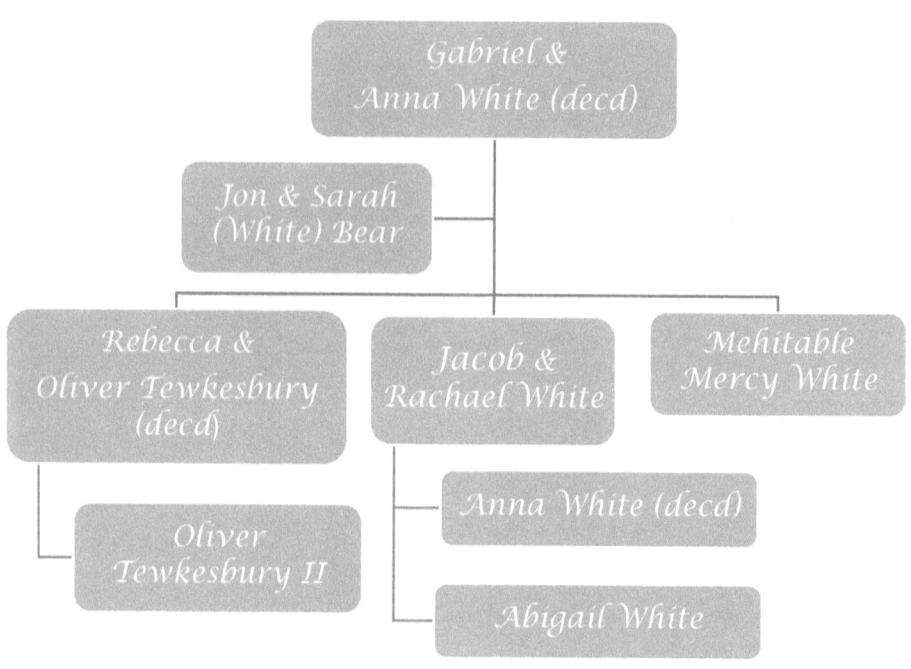

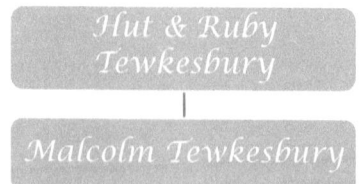

Dedicated in memory of
My loving grandmother—my north star,
Josephine Elizabeth Burke

Chapter 1

Hut felt the warm trickle of blood drip from the corner of his mouth as he bit down harder on the knife blade between his teeth. He held his body in place, both hands grasping a stern line, feet braced against the ship's port side, waiting in the darkness for the signal. Staring down the ship's gunwales, he could barely make out where Jacob also waited. Only, Jacob held fast with one hand and one serviceable hook, courtesy of the Continental Army's surgeon who had fitted him a year after he lost his left arm just below the elbow. Jacob hadn't paid the "ultimate price" the revolution had exacted from so many others, but he paid a hefty price at the age of 15, so young a soldier. Four years later, the hook replacement never impeded him. In fact, his ability to grasp and hook onto the side of any ship was a desirable and needed skill for a privateer.

The knife dug deeper into the corner of Hut's mouth as an unexpected wave rolled the ship slightly. His body swung away, but immediately returned to the ship's side, feet braced again. He glanced down at the black, murky water just ten feet below, and a chill deepened within him.

His mind drifted back to the moment he had been recruited by Captain Treadwell two months earlier.

"Strapping," Captain Treadwell had exclaimed to his old friend, Gabriel White. Gabriel's son, Jacob, looked on as the four of them stood on the deck of the sloop, *Josephine*. The captain had circled Hut while the former Negro slave stood still as a statue, only his eyes shifting side to side, wondering what would become of him. Hut stood six feet tall with broad shoulders, wiry pitch-black hair and eyes black as cannon balls.

"I can vouch for him is what I'm saying, Captain," Gabriel chimed in.

"Me as well," Jacob exclaimed.

Hut had thrown father and son questioning looks.

"Can you write? Keep a log?" Treadwell grilled as he stared into Hut's eyes.

"Yessa," Hut replied. "Miss Mehti taught me to write over a year ago."

"Can you navigate by the stars?"

"He made his way under darkness from Richmond to Valley Forge by the stars," Gabriel answered. "And that ought to be good enough."

"You look mighty strong, I'll give you that. What do you say to being my first mate? You'll share in the spoils. Privateering isn't for everyone, but people around here will be calling you 'sir.'"

Hut recalled being speechless, unsure if he was hearing correctly. Then a smile as wide as Long Island Sound crossed his face. "Yessa, I think I'd like dat."

Captain Treadwell reached across and shook hands with his new first mate, Hut Tewkesbury.

"Jus one ting, Captain. We got to keep this here boat afloat 'cause I can't swim." The men all chuckled at Hut's revelation.

Holding tight to the stern line, that introduction held fast in his memory now, as it always did when he was on the waters. *Maybe one day Mehti could teach me to swim, too.*

Their tethered Boston whaler floated alongside the British brig, awaiting the end of the assault. If successful, they would capture the crew and sail the brig into New London harbor, approximately four nautical miles to the northeast. The only disadvantage of the eight-man assault team was their fatigue after rowing the distance through the darkness out of Old Saybrook. Luckily, their spyglass kept the brig in sight.

Hut heard voices on deck, but at this time of night most of the Brits would be in their bunks, with only a few watchmen up top. An easy target. There was no way of knowing what cargo was on board, but each prize they'd taken in the last two months had proved profitable, and not one man had been lost—so far.

Hut watched as the final privateer got into position. Then came the whistle from Captain Treadwell, and all eight men began to scramble up and over, landing simultaneously on the deck. Hut found himself behind a young British sailor who turned toward him, startled. With his knife in one hand and a pistol in the other, Hut bore down with all his might, the butt of his pistol cracking the forehead of the stunned sailor. Jacob landed not too far away, near a second sailor. Lowering his body to a crouch, he spun around and swung his arm out, grappling the sailor's calf with his hook, causing him to fall to his knees, screaming in agony. No other sailors were on deck.

Captain Treadwell swiftly followed four of his men below deck in search of the ship's captain who—along with several other Brits, upon hearing the commotion—were stumbling from their bunks and heading toward them. But Treadwell and his men had their guns cocked and raised, confronting their enemies mid-ship.

"Good evening, Captain," Treadwell addressed the man who seemed to be the ranking officer. "I believe we have just taken over your ship. I require that you drop your weapons."

The British sailors looked at one another, then toward their captain and, seeing his nod, dropped their weapons onto the deck below.

"Check the cargo, lads," Treadwell called out to two more men entering the hold. Lanterns in hand, the men scattered in different directions of the hold to investigate.

"How many on board?" Treadwell asked the commanding officer.

"Eighteen," was the Brit's reply, his expression betraying a combination of resignation, humiliation and anger, his hands limp in the air.

"Round 'em up, men," Treadwell ordered. Then he turned to the captain. "After you." Motioning forward, he stood aside to allow his captives to begin their ascent to the main deck. Once there, Treadwell's men secured their captives to the two main masts and the deck rails.

"Captain Treadwell," one of the privateers called out from the hatchway. "We have a twondozen pigs, several barrels of molasses, flour and numerous casks of rum."

"Pirates!" the British captain scoffed at Treadwell as he was lowered to the deck floor to be secured to the mast, his hands tied behind him.

"Pirates? I beg to differ. We are gentlemen privateers," Treadwell responded. He reached into his shirt pocket and produced his Letter of Marque. He unfolded it and held it within inches of the captain's face.

"Pirates, hooligans and traitors!" yelled the captain, his face crimson with fury. He spat on the document.

"Calm yourself, sir, and enjoy the cruise to New London," Treadwell responded. Then to his men he shouted, "Weigh anchor!"

A slight southwesterly breeze allowed a slow sail to their home port, but at least the wind was in their favor. The pre-dawn light gave glimpses of calming waters and a whitewashed pale-blue sky.

Chapter 2

From the moment Gabriel White's daughter, Mehitable Mercy White, was born, he knew she would be a willful child. Granville's midwife, Goody Beckham, blamed Mehitable's infant irritability on colic. But Gabriel thought differently. Unlike his oldest daughter, Rebecca, who was now a mother herself, Mehti, as she became known, marched to the beat of a drummer that perhaps only their Indian farmhand, Jon Bear, could understand. To Gabriel's mind, the child took after neither him nor his late wife, Anna.

Gabriel ruminated now as he sat on the stoop of their barn-red farmhouse that stood on the west side of the Granville green. Rebecca was always a calming, stable influence on the family and an exemplary mother to her son, Oliver Tewkesbury II. Gabriel had been concerned when Rebecca's short-lived marriage ended with the death of her husband, Oliver, in the Battle of Monmouth. He felt certain she would have difficulty resuming a normal life. It would have been so easy for her to slip into depression – as her mother had done before dying by her own hand. But Rebecca was resilient and poured all her love and energy into the rearing of little Oliver, just two years old now.

Fourteen-year-old Mehti, at the moment, was nowhere to be found, and not for the first time. *She worries my soul,* Gabriel thought. He realized he was grinding his teeth and quickly stopped.

He glanced up when he heard Oliver's cackling giggle. The toddler trotted across the green, his bouncing blond curls glimmering in the sunlight, Rebecca at his heels. She scooped Oliver up, twirled him around as he chortled in glee, and sat down next to her father, placing the boy on her lap.

Rebecca's gaze shifted slightly upward, toward Gabriel's furrowed brow. "What has you in such a contemplative mood, Father?" she asked.

"It's Mehti... again. I don't think she came home last night. Did you happen to see her? I retired early and she still had not returned from her supposed hunt. When I checked in on her this morning, it appeared her bed had not been slept in."

"Father, you worry too much after Mehti. You know she can be trusted to take care of herself. I feel certain she is fine, but if you'd like, I will talk with Jon Bear. Perhaps he knows her whereabouts."

"Her thirst for adventure tries my nerves incessantly," Gabriel growled in discontent.

"But, Father, she does all her chores, keeps the garden and kitchen, and has shown enthusiasm for Schoolmaster Greeley's tutelage an evening a week. She even practices her stitches, even though it is a chore to her. What more can a father ask? And she's reached womanhood, Father. That should calm her into maturity."

"And her womanhood worries me all the more. And Greeley is a whole other matter. I'm surprised you brought him up. Have you given him any further thought?"

Mordecai Greeley, an educated man of means twice Rebecca's age, had approached Gabriel, expressing interest in courting his daughter. Although Greeley was not an unattractive man, his pinched features and fastidious nervous nature lent no appeal to Rebecca. Every time she looked at him and tried to consider him as a spouse, her mind would drift back to memories of her handsome Oliver with his kind, gentle ways. The warmth of his lovely grey eyes and soothing countenance would melt her heart – unlike Greeley's prickly, flinching mannerisms. Rebecca felt sorry for Greeley, as she knew he was all too aware of his lack of appeal. But she didn't feel sorry enough to regard him as a suitor.

"I know we've had this discussion before, Rebecca, but you're going on twenty-four, with a young son who needs a father. Your future is at stake. I have no intention of marrying again at my age, and I appreciate your position as mistress in this household. But you must think of your future."

As if he were summoned by the conversation, Mordecai Greeley came strolling down the lane, accompanied by his walking stick. His countenance was tall and slender, his chest somewhat concave and shoulders stooped, a defeated look about him. Greeley tipped his hat as he approached, revealing graying temples and a receding hairline. An inadequate stringy tail of dull blackish hair was tied at the nape of his crane-like, angled neck. His intense blue eyes were striking, but held an iciness that always caused Rebecca to avert her eyes. He usually wore a long, black dress coat – even on the hottest of days. And unlike most of the men of Granville, he was always clean shaven, even in winter.

"Good afternoon to you, Gabriel," Mordecai intoned dully. Turning to Rebecca, his eyes lingered a bit longer. "And top of the day to you, Mrs. Tewkesbury. A fine day for a stroll, don't you think?"

"Indeed, Mr. Greeley. You must thoroughly enjoy this lovely day."

"Your company would make it perfect, with your father's permission."

"His permission is not necessary," Rebecca replied more tartly than she intended, her chin slightly elevated. "I am widowed, as you know, and can speak for myself. As to your suggestion, I have much to do on this day, so if you'll excuse me." She lifted Oliver and stood to leave.

No sooner had those words come out of her mouth than the three of them turned toward the sound of an approaching wagon. Shielding her eyes from the sunlight, Rebecca watched Jacob's wagon approach over the horizon. He and Hut had been gone for almost a week to help plan and execute their latest intervention with any cargo-laden British vessel cruising the Sound and bound for Long Island or New York City, both occupied by the British Army.

Rebecca and Gabriel breathed a sigh of relief at the sight of Jacob and Hut. Greeley hung his head even lower, simultaneously peeved and dejected at the interruption.

Mordecai Greeley could never accept the story behind how Hut Tewkesbury assumed that surname. Nor could he understand how this former slave managed to wheedle his way into the good graces of the White family. But he intended to hold his counsel on the matter in order to remain on good terms with Gabriel – who had some inexplicable fondness for the black man. At some point in time, when it was more appropriate and he had command of the situation, Greeley determined he would investigate further and make whatever changes to the family structure were necessary.

Hut pulled the rig up to the front of the farmhouse; he and Jacob leapt down from the front seat.

"So good to see you both back again, safe and sound," Gabriel said, patting them both on the back. "What have you brought us this time?"

The three men, followed by Rebecca and her son, moved to the back of the wagon as Mordecai observed from a distance.

"I think dis will please you," Hut exclaimed as he pulled back the tarp and revealed their share of the haul from their night raid on the British brig—a cask of rum and a barrel of flour. Hitched to the wagon's railing was a piglet, its pink snout held high, curiously sniffing the air.

"A respectable haul," Gabriel commented as he smiled at both of them. "And what of the captives? Were there any?"

"Eighteen captives including the captain," Hut smiled. "Dey be held at the jail in New London. I 'spect dey be traded for some of our own. The bulk of the cargo is being sent on to the troops in New Jersey."

"Excellent!" Gabriel exclaimed.

"I'm so proud of you," Rebecca said to her brother Jacob as she hugged him with Oliver in her arms. Caught up in the moment, Oliver also leaned in and hugged his uncle.

"This was probably one of our easiest claims," Jacob explained. "We caught them unawares." Turning to his father, Jacob asked, "Shall we butcher this piglet for dinner in celebration?"

Gabriel looked to Mordecai to ask his opinion on the matter, but their visitor had, without a word, already taken his leave and was headed down the lane toward the other side of the green.

"Let us fatten this animal up and save butchering for late fall. Smoked, he'll help sustain us through the winter. I'll ask Jon

Bear to build him a pen, lest he go foraging in the woods and end up on somebody else's table."

Chapter 3

Mehti squirmed a bit to relieve the pain sitting for hours on a burly, knotted driftwood log had caused her bottom side. She lifted her rump slightly to reposition her skirts and felt immediate relief. Again, she peered through the spyglass, one of only three she knew of in New London County, and appreciated that she was entrusted with the care for so precious an instrument. Nathaniel Shaw, Jr., Connecticut's Naval Agent, had allowed her to use it on her missions, and she had no intention of letting him down by allowing any harm come to the glass. Her focus was interrupted by an abrupt nudge on her right side.

"Stop bumping into me!" Mehti scolded her tag-along spying companion, 16-year-old Caleb Rogers. She always envied that he wore breeches, something her father would never allow her to do.

"Sorry," Caleb responded sheepishly.

Caleb took every opportunity to venture out with Mehti, and would further attempt inadvertent physical contact whenever possible, which mostly annoyed her. When walking down the lane together, he would always stumble into her apologetically. In her father's kitchen as she prepared lemonade, he would lean in, claiming he just wanted to watch her prepare the drink, just another opportunity to brush up to her side. Then there were their horseback rides in to New London to signal news, or their return ride to Granville, twenty miles north of the coast. Their physical proximity struck Mehti simultaneously as both comfort and discomfort. But when it came to her ship-monitoring forays along the waterfront, Caleb's company was welcome because, after all, solo spying could be a lonely business.

Mehti and Caleb sat on the storm-strewn log at General Neck beach head as early-spring breezes floated up off Long Island Sound and swept, cool and soft, across their faces. Seagulls swooped and dove for fish while plovers skittered along the water's edge. The musty smell of salt marsh at low tide permeated the air. Together they had watched the sun rise over Groton point just an hour earlier and already its heat began to warm them, a hope for comfortable weather coming.

In the eerie pre-dawn light, Mehti had been elated to spy a British brig sailing into New London harbor. When the ship was in closer view, she made out both Hut and her brother on deck. A surge of pride coursed through her veins. It was Jacob and Hut's third successful haul. With each commandeered vessel, a sense of confidence built among the privateers, affirming the patriots would eventually prevail in the revolution. Mehti's first glimpse of Hut and Jacob caused her to jump up and cheer, with Caleb following her lead.

"They've done it, Caleb!" Mehti screeched.

"Well, I'm definitely pleased, Mehti," Caleb responded in his usual calming tone.

Mehti momentarily reflected on their awkward – and, thankfully, short-lived – hug of celebration. She wondered now what her father would say, had he known she was not only out all night, but in the company of Caleb Rogers, even as innocent as it was.

With his tousled blond curls, Caleb Rogers stood a full head taller than Mehti. But she was the bolder of the two. She attributed Caleb's passive nature to his Quaker upbringing, since he was one of the numerous Rogerene Quakers who hailed from the section of town known as Quaker Hill. Named for their religious patriarch, John Rogers, the Rogerenes had a reputation for their cantankerous activities, more so than the docility one might expect from a religion that touts pacifism. Many of the local Rogerenes had removed themselves to New Jersey generations ago. But their reputation as egalitarians, often treating slaves as equals, along with their refusal to honor the Sabbath by working when they pleased, still lingered to this day. Even slaves were allowed to worship among them, which rankled the Congregationalists. Evidence of the Rogerenes' strong previous presence could be witnessed among the numerous unmarked burial stones that pockmarked the grounds near upper Mamacoke on the banks of the Thames as it gently and respectfully rolled past.

"Mehti, we should get you back home. Your father's going to discover your absence and I would not want to experience his reaction when he finds out."

"I can take care of Father," Mehti answered assuredly. "I'm sure Hut and Jon Bear will vouch for me and my activities, should it come to that. After all, I'm helping the cause. If we can identify British vessels heading for New York City, we can intercept them further down the Sound."

"Regardless, we'd best get moving. I don't think your father would approve of you staying out all night, especially with me," Caleb said with a slight smile of accomplishment.

"That's precisely why I'm going to drop you off just outside of Granville. You can walk the few miles home from there. No one need ever know, unless you expose us," Mehti said with a glare. She stood and turned to gather her chestnut mare, Maisey, grazing nearby.

Ever since Hut had assumed the role of First Mate on the *Josephine,* it had been Mehti's dream to join him and Jacob in their privateering adventures onboard the fast-moving sloop. She fantasized herself, disguised as a cabin boy, gaining employment on a British ship and easily causing a diversion while patriots swooped up and over a vessel's railings. Or, better yet, she could seek passage on a vessel as a beautiful, mysterious damsel in distress, then lure a ship's captain to his capture by her signal alone.

After all, Mehti was fourteen now and a shapely and comely young lady who could wield her feminine wiles if she needed to. Her figure had filled out nicely and her hair, while not quite as pretty Rebecca's, had grown just as long, with soft light-brown tresses that gently fell about her face when she wore it down.

"Do you think I'm pretty?" she asked suddenly as she spun around to face Caleb.

Caleb swallowed hard, but did not answer.

"So, you have to think about it?" Mehti asked, exposing her disappointment.

"No, no," Caleb stuttered. "I think you're the most beautiful girl in Granville."

"Just in Granville?"

"Mehti, you're the most beautiful girl I've ever seen," Caleb responded with all the emphasis he could marshal to assure her of his sincerity.

She responded with a nod of satisfaction, then swiftly turned again to mount Maisey.

"Help me up, Caleb."

Caleb bent over, cradling her boot in his hands, and gave Mehti a hoist up onto her horse that she immodestly straddled by hiking up her skirts. Then she reached down and lent her hand to help lift Caleb up behind her. While it was more traditional for a woman to ride behind a man, Mehti always liked to ride in front.

If they made good time, they would arrive in Granville in a few hours.

Chapter 4

The White household and surrounds had become well occupied since several family members made their way to Valley Forge and back two years prior. Young Master Oliver scurried across the floors with the energy of a bear cub. The family watched in amazement as the strong, agile child jumped, ran and climbed his way in every direction as if the world were merely a play area under his command. At two years old, he could already be described as handsome.

The rest of the household included the patriarch, Gabriel; his daughter Rebecca; son Jacob and wife Rachael and their angelic and elfin three-year-old daughter, Abigail. Abigail was a wisp of a child who learned early on to step aside or find the corner of any room whenever Oliver was wielding his toddler powers. And of course the ever-moving Mehti kept a semi-presence with her comings and goings.

The crimson barn now had two lean-tos, each built off opposite sides. One side was home to the Whites' Indian farmhand, Jon Bear and his wife, Sarah, Gabriel's sister. The other housed Hut, his wife, Ruby, and their three-month-old son, Malcolm – a name Hut had chosen.

"I like Malcolm, Ruby. Malcolm is a name dat people will look up to. It's the name for a man who could be his own man. I like that kind of name for our son."

And Ruby agreed. Malcolm was precious because after his difficult birth, and after the laudanum wore off, midwife Margaret Beckham informed Ruby she would not be able to have another child. The doctor had been called in from Norwich to perform necessary surgery to save Ruby's life.

"Don't you fret none, Ruby," Hut told her, knowing she wanted a large family like the one she was born into.

"Dis be my only chile," Ruby told him, as she gazed lovingly at the sleeping swaddled face of Malcolm with his charcoal-black eyelashes. One small tear rolled down her coffee-colored cheek. "My family was big, but we be scattered across many plantations, so what good it do? This one, free chile will be by our side and that be good enough for me."

The business of the household was on Mehti's mind as she brought Maisey around the back side of the barn and deftly removed her bridle and led her to her stall. Maisey immediately found the bucket of water stationed in the stall's corner. Exiting the barn, Mehti looked in both directions and, seeing no one about, lifted her skirts and scurried across to the back of the house, entering through the side kitchen door. Rebecca stood at the sink washing baby carrots and humming contentedly to herself, when Mehti's entrance startled her.

"Mehti, you gave me such a start," Rebecca exclaimed. Baby Oliver sat on the floor by his mother's side, ripping the green tops from the harvested carrots and handing them up to his mother.

Gabriel entered the kitchen from the sitting room. "Mehti, where have you been?" he demanded.

"I rose before you, Father. It's already been a busy day for me," Mehti responded as she sashayed past him. "I've been on the green, cooking for the men," she lied with a nonchalant glance. Passing through the kitchen like a summer breeze, she headed upstairs before her father could ask her any additional questions.

Gabriel rubbed his salt-and-pepper beard, a look of worry on his face. He felt his age in his bones and in his mind every time he contemplated the difficulties he faced keeping up with the activities of his youngest daughter. Rebecca was a different story. He knew he need not worry after Rebecca. But there was much about his oldest daughter Gabriel did not know. In fact, no one did.

Rebecca's change came about on a late-fall day the prior year. Little Oliver had been put down for his afternoon nap and Rebecca decided to cross the green to the general store to pick up a few staples. She grabbed her cloak and basket and headed out along the roadway that ran between the green and a large field that skirted its western border.

The town green had daily been a flurry of activity ever since some 220 French allies –Hussars, horsemen under the command of one Armand Louis de Gontaut, duc de Lauzun, had arrived in early November. The log cabins that spotted the green in neat rows reminded her of her stay at Valley Forge. She knew the camp life quite well and, therefore, avoided the area as much as possible, while Mehti was constantly among the French troops, assisting in any way she could. Lauzun now occupied the largest home in Granville, the Redcoach Inn, positioned opposite the southwest corner of the green. The war office, also located on the edge of the green, saw constant traffic with couriers on horseback dismounting briefly to deliver or retrieve messages of military import, then immediately remounting and galloping on their way.

That late-fall day was no exception and Rebecca strode past all the activity, determined to complete her errands and return home before Oliver awoke. To the north, the aroma of baking bread emanated from the army's newly built brick ovens and wafted its way down the green. A light snow of disparate flakes began to lazily make their way to the ground, a first sign of winter weather. Rebecca glanced out across the field, her attention captured by a lone, mounted Hussar commanding his horse through maneuvers, then charging the animal at full speed, only to have it stop short, rear up and turn back to repeat the drill. She was captivated by both the strength and power of the beautiful animal as well as the skill of the horseman. Her stubborn gaze pulled her from the roadway like a tether and out into the field, where she stood like an enchanted statue.

On his return ride, the Hussar finally noticed Rebecca and stopped mid-field, his stare taking hold of the other end of her imaginary tether. His horse stomped in disapproval, its nostrils spewing clouds of vapor as he exhaled, eager to continue their run. After a brief pause, the Hussar turned his horse toward Rebecca and unhurriedly walked the animal toward her.

And that was the moment Rebecca would never forget as long as she lived—the moment that caused her to gasp every time it surfaced in her memory. The French Hussar stood tall and majestic in his saddle, his blue uniform setting off soft grey eyes that locked onto Rebecca's. She wondered whether he would speak to her, then thought perhaps he did not speak English. But it didn't matter, as words suddenly seemed so unnecessary. His dashing looks caused her to tremble with caution, but only momentarily. A beautiful smile crossed his face as he removed his foot from his stirrup and reached down, offering his gloved hand to her, his eyes never leaving hers.

Rebecca did not hesitate. She set down her basket and, inserting her boot into the stirrup, reached up and grabbed the soldier's hand as he hoisted her up behind him, side saddle. The horse cocked its ears as if in disbelief. Instinctively, Rebecca wrapped her arms around the soldier's waist and immediately welcomed the warmth of his body. He said something to her in French that she did not understand but took to mean, "Hold on."

The Hussar turned his horse back to the field, circling it at a slow trot, twice around, a ride Rebecca wished would never end. But of course it did end, and the soldier brought her back to their meeting place all too soon. He elegantly swung his leg over the horse's head, a move that would seem awkward for any mere mortal, and dismounted. He reached up and wrapped his hands around Rebecca's trim waist and lifted her off the horse as if she were light mist and let her feet return gently to the earth. He held her gaze like a prized possession, then tipped his festooned hat.

"Merci," he said with a voice that could melt snow.

"Merci."

She turned to go, but could not help turning back several times to make sure he was real and what she had just experienced was not a dream. He never took his eyes off her until she disappeared across the green.

Rebecca reflected on that day now as she stood at the kitchen sink, humming through her chores. There was a saying among the women of Granville: "The Hussars are loved by every wife." Rebecca felt joy in her heart for her gallant Hussar she came to know as Frederic Dubois, who had been a part of her life for the last few months, unbeknownst to anyone – but her joy was pierced when she was struck with the realization of his inevitable departure. At some point this summer, the Hussars would be moving on to join up with the Continental Army.

Rebecca felt it was time her relationship with Frederic came out of the shadows. She would talk to her father and ask if he would mind if she had a soldier friend over for dinner. After all, the Hussars were a poorly paid lot whose food rations over the winter were sparse. She would appear a compassionate soul in her father's eyes if she were to invite a soldier to dine with them. Even though some of the Hussars had violated local hospitality and irritated many a Granville resident by stealing chickens, cutting down trees or removing fences for fire wood, her father viewed them in good stead.

Chapter 5

One or two days a week, Hut traversed the pitted roadway by donkey from Granville to New London to ply his butchering skills in the rear pantry of the local grocery store on Water Street. In the months he spent at Valley Forge, slaughtering and butchering cattle and hogs had been his primary task, his strength and agility suiting him well for the job. His current employer, old man Cuthbert, was no longer able to physically manage the rigors of butchering and was, therefore, amenable to hiring Hut, as long as he kept to the barn and the pantry.

The first day Gabriel brought Hut to meet Cuthbert to discuss a possible job, the old man made his expectations of Hut quite clear. The three met around the back of the store, adjacent to a temporary holding pen for livestock awaiting their fate. Bent over like a gnarled tree branch, scrawny and unable to fully extend his crumpled frame, Cuthbert stared down at the ground. So stooped was he, looking a man in the eye had become a strenuous chore.

"I can't pay much. Maybe half the usual. And you'd have to stay out of sight. Some whites won't like knowing their meat's been handled by a black man. No, that won't do," Cuthbert said straightforward as he strained to right himself and look directly at Hut. "And it ain't nobody's business what I'm paying you. Got that?

Folks complain niggers willing to work for less are taking work from them. This here's between you and me and nobody else. You got that? You come in through the back, do your butchering and leave through the back. That's all I can do." Cuthbert leaned to the left and spit tobacco juice within inches of Hut's feet.

Gabriel glanced at Hut to gauge his reaction.

"Dat be good for me," Hut responded then put out his hand to seal the understanding. Cuthbert waved it away.

"No need for that. Just be here first thing in the morning. As you can see, we've got a few animals waiting for slaughter." Cuthbert motioned over to the pen. "You do chickens and turkeys, too?" he asked as an afterthought.

"Sure," Hut replied.

"Good," Cuthbert replied. Without another word, he spun on his heel and headed back into his store.

"It's a start," Gabriel told Hut as he patted him on the back. "Between your privateering, working the farm and butchering here, I think you can get ahead a bit."

Hut preferred privateering above all else because on the open seas, for some reason he did not quite understand, he was treated differently than on land. As the first mate, he had a certain status among his peers. Maybe it had to do with the life–or-death scenarios that always played out on the waters. When a soldier or privateer needed to depend on his shipmate to protect him, the color of his skin didn't make any difference. The code of honor and ethics shifted dramatically on the open seas. Everyone knew they had to depend on one another, regardless of rank, position, age or skin color.

On land, it was a different story. From the time Hut arrived in Granville with Gabriel and Rebecca after they returned from Valley Forge, Gabriel had introduced him to a community that was, overall, quite welcoming. Hut was grateful that his son, Malcolm, would grow up in such a community. But on land in general, Hut was viewed as a lesser man—had to know his place as a lesser man. And he had no idea whether that would, or could, ever change. His mammy always taught him to be grateful and to praise the Lord for every day. The prospects of his life had improved dramatically since his release from life as a slave in Richmond and joining the Continental Army, even if ever so briefly. He would be forever grateful for being taken in by the White family and coming to Granville. Most days he could scarcely believe his good fortune.

On Sundays the entire White family attended the First Congregational church on the green. While there were few blacks in Granville, those who attended church sat in the loft. Catholic French soldiers often attended services since it was the only nearby church, but they sat toward the back of the sanctuary, in deference to the locals.

When Gabriel, Jon Bear, Jacob and Hut went to White Horse Tavern, Hut and Jon Bear usually kept to the corners of the room, while Gabriel and Jacob would seat themselves at a center table or stand at the bar. When the French first arrived in Granville, the tavern was a throng of much clinking of tankards and overall jubilation. It surprised Hut that French soldiers who spoke some English, took orders in German and swore in Hungarian, would openly approach him and engage him in conversation. But the tenor and tone toward French encampment had changed dramatically over the winter as resources needed to support the soldiers were exhausted and many took to thievery from the locals.

"They go too far," Hut observed a farmer exclaim one Saturday night while imbibing at the White Horse. "Four of my best hens have gone missing." Several French soldiers at the tavern turned toward the farmer, then nonchalantly turned away. Their dismissive nature irked the farmer even more and he began marching toward them, his fury evident. But he was stopped midway by a few of the townsmen.

"Calm yourself," one of them advised. "We don't need any trouble in here. You have to speak to the councilmen and get this straightened out."

"Rubbish!" the farmer spat. "They'll do nothing and neither will Lauzun."

"Count your blessings. The way the women swoon over these Hussars, one could be forced to end up with an unwanted son-in-law."

Many heads turned at that comment, and no sooner had the words been spoken than the farmer realized the looseness of his tongue and also turned away. The flurry of tension dissipated as swiftly as it had started.

Chapter 6

Throughout the winter and early spring of the year, it had been Rebecca's joy to engage in occasional trysts with Frederic through the countryside to any place they could be alone. More often than not, they met on the green. After their first meeting, that snowy November day when he rode her on his horse, Rebecca made it a point to volunteer to run errands across the green whenever supplies were needed at home, no matter how bad the weather. Or if there was the slightest mention there may be news of the war posted at the tavern, she was eager to trek across the green to read the details. It didn't take long before she again ran into Frederic, who seemed just as eager to cross her path.

At their second meeting, Frederic was accompanied by one of his cabin mates, Claude, a rascally Frenchman who fortunately also spoke German and some English. When Frederic saw Rebecca trudging through the snow across the green on a crisp clear morning, he grabbed Claude by the arm and steered him in her direction. Again, as with their first meeting, their eyes locked and the world fell away momentarily until Claude cleared his throat to remind them of his presence.

"Bon jour, mademoiselle. My name is Claude Boisvert," he said as he removed his hat and made a slight bow. "Frederic is one of my cabin mates."

Rebecca clasped her hands in glee. "How wonderful that you speak English," she exclaimed.

"It is good to meet you. I have heard about your encounter with Frederic. If I may be so bold, I anticipate he would welcome an opportunity to see you again, if that is favorable to you." Then he turned to Frederic who stood hopefully by, waiting to understand what had transpired and delivered the translation of his invitation. Frederic read Rebecca's response by the smile that instantly lit up her face. She dared not a moment of pretense, knowing their potential time together would be ending all too soon. While an exact date for the troops' departure had not been decided, it was anticipated they would be leaving Granville sometime in early summer.

"I would very much like that," she said speaking directly to Frederic.

Claude cleared his throat again. "I have been trying to teach Frederic English and he has done well, but I believe he could use more personal tutelage," Claude continued, a slight twinkle in his eye.

And so it began that Rebecca would find whatever moments she could to meet with Frederic under the guise of English lessons. He learned quickly. In the process, she learned much about him as well. He hailed from Alsace, as did Claude. He had been a soldier for two years and, much to her dismay, came to

America not to support their noble cause, but to defeat the British wherever they were engaged. Anti-British sentiment ran deep among all of Lauzun's men, as well as with Lauzun. Their hatred of the British was rooted in the humiliation the House of Bourbon faced with the Treaty of Paris in 1763 that ended the Seven Years' War and sealed France's defeat and Britain's dominance. Frederic, now 26 years of age, had grown up with the bitter taste of that defeat, as did all of his fellow soldiers.

"We fight for France," he told her one day, as his expression went from one of gentle attentiveness to deep resolve.

Rebecca surmised from Frederic's reserved and polite nature that he was a gentleman soldier from the middle classes, which was quite the opposite from the British rank and file who hailed primarily from poorhouses and prisons. The dregs of Britain's society made up the bulk of British soldiery, as they often signed away their life to gain their freedom. Not so with the French military, and Frederic was evidence of that fact.

Frederic, in turn, learned of Rebecca's life.

"I really must be getting home," she said at one of their earlier meetings as they sat by one of the fires ever present on the green during the cold weather. Rebecca and Frederic were rarely alone, as soldiers continually wandered the green out of boredom. Some would sneak off on a hunt chasing after whatever wildlife they could find to bring back to camp and cook on a spit. Hunting had been officially banned by their commander after an incident that took place the previous November just after their arrival. To celebrate the feast day of Saint Hubert, the patron saint of hunters, a number of men took off on a traditional hunt with horses and hounds that resulted in numerous irate farmers whose fields, planted with winter rye, were trampled.

But with the coming of spring, the weather had warmed, and melted snow left the green muddied and difficult to navigate, which did not stop either Rebecca or Frederic from their lessons. At the end of a lengthy session, Rebecca hastily said, "I really must go. My aunt Sarah is caring for Oliver and I do not want to take advantage of her kind nature."

"Oliver?" Frederic asked.

"Yes," she said, hesitating. "My son, Oliver. My husband..." she began and then hesitated again. Rebecca found it painful to find the words to describe her loss of Oliver to Frederic. Not only was it emotionally hard, but so much could be lost in her explanation due to their language barrier. She chose her words carefully and spoke slowly, which also helped her maintain composure.

"My husband, Oliver's namesake, was killed at the Battle of Monmouth Courthouse in New Jersey two years ago. We were married only briefly but we were very much in love." Frederic seemed saddened by her revelation. At the same time, he seemed to absorb some of the suffering of her loss. "I think you are very much like him." She reached up and touched his face. "You have the same eyes," she said softly. Their touch caused a rush of feeling across her entire body, and she sensed Frederic felt it too. But she was uncertain what his response would be.

Frederic's soft grey eyes hardened momentarily as he took her hands in his. "Now I have another reason to fight the British," he said, a blond tendril of hair falling across his face as he bent down and kissed her hands.

Rebecca felt like a barrier between them had been lifted, and everything seemed possible in what previously seemed impossible.

Chapter 7

After church on Sundays, the White family often gathered for a meal, followed by a time for readings, reflection and conversation in the farmhouse parlor once Oliver and Abigail had been put down for their afternoon naps. Generally, either Gabriel, Rebecca or Jacob would take turns reading to the family from the *Bible* or *Poor Richard's Almanac*. Often discussion turned to the war, and most frequently they talked about Benedict Arnold's treasonous acts, a continual topic among Granville town folk.

While Gabriel had never met Benedict Arnold, many in Granville had associations with him during his lawyering years in Norwich, just ten miles away and the place of Arnold's birth. The betrayal felt by patriots in eastern Connecticut, and indeed across the colonies, ran deep. Arnold had turned redcoat on September 21, 1780, the previous fall, when his plans to turn over West Point to the British failed and he escaped to a British vessel anchored in waters nearby. The shock of his defection still had not worn off. On the town green, a straw-stuffed dummy of Arnold had been burned in effigy, the enraged crowd pounding their fists in the air, chanting, "Traitor, traitor!" The hanging effigy burned out and fell to the ground, only to be stomped repeatedly by townspeople. Even several months later, Arnold was all residents wanted to talk about. And Gabriel's family was no exception.

Sitting by the crackling fire, Gabriel reflected on how crowded the room had become, now that their family had grown so much. He looked around the room at Jacob and Rachael, Hut and Ruby, Jon Bear and Sarah, and Mehti and Rebecca. He recalled the days when Sunday meals included only him, Anna and their three children. He considered it glorious and bountiful providence to be surrounded with so large and comforting a family.

It was at such a gathering that Rebecca decided to bring up the subject of inviting Frederic to dinner at their next Sunday meal. She wanted everyone's concurrence and support, so it was helpful that all were present.

"Father," Rebecca began as she laid her stitching down on her lap and caught his attention. "I have a wonderful suggestion I'd like to make."

"Oh? And what would that be, Rebecca?" he asked, as he stood and stoked the fire, then, returning to his wing back chair, lifted his horn to his ear to better hear her from across the room. At the Battle of Monmouth Courthouse, Gabriel had lost much of his hearing due to his proximity to a cannon blast.

"I am sure you are all aware of the suffering the Hussars have faced since coming to Granville. Their rations are slight and meals sparse." She glanced around the room, seeking approval. Jon Bear, Sarah and Mehti were nodding in agreement, but her father sat stern, leaning in to hear her better. "I have made a friend among the troops and thought it we would be of kind spirit to invite him for dinner next Sunday. In fact, he has a cabin mate we could also invite, if we feel particularly generous."

Mehti spoke up. "Is this the gentleman I've seen you with on the green? The tall one with blond hair?"

Gabriel raised a brow. Rebecca blushed slightly. "Oh, why, yes. You must have seen me giving English lessons as I have been prone to do to help soldiers communicate better with the locals."

"I think it's a splendid idea," Jacob said. "I realize their presence has been difficult at times, but after all, they are here to support us and we should do what we can to support them in return. Many of the officers have been put up by our neighbors. I should think it's the least we can do to have two of them for dinner. In fact, I propose we have them over every Sunday until they leave, which won't be in the too distant future, I suppose."

"You are so right, Jacob," Mehti agreed. "So shall we have them to dinner, next Sunday?" Mehti put the question to her father. The entire discussion had gone much better than Rebecca had ever expected.

Gabriel seemed to be mulling it over, then nodded in agreement. "Very well. We'll set out the extra table and Rebecca, please extend an invitation on our behalf."

"Splendid," Rebecca said, and a pleased look lit upon her face.

The afternoon was waning and they were each preparing to depart the room when a knock came on the front door. Jacob answered it as all heads turned to see who would be calling at this unusual time of day.

"Ah, Mr. Greeley. And how are you this fine day?" Jacob asked.

"I am quite well, Jacob. I wonder if your father and sister are home as I have some business to discuss with them." Jacob turned to his family.

"We are just leaving," Jon Bear said as he grabbed his hat and coat and headed for the door, bypassing Jacob.

"And we be leaving, too," Hut said, cradling a sleeping Malcolm as he and Ruby also bypassed Jacob and scurried out the door. The room was empty in no time.

"Might I come in?" Greeley asked.

Gabriel stood. "Mordecai, please come in," Gabriel said, offering him a chair. There was an air of tension and expectation as Mordecai sat in a ladder-back chair, his stooped shoulders defying the chair's straight form.

"We'll just be upstairs," Rachael said to her father-in-law, taking Jacob by the hand. "And we'll tend to Oliver, should he wake up before your visit is over."

"Mehti, don't you have an errand to run?" Gabriel asked.

"No, Father."

40

"Or perhaps you'd like to tidy up in the kitchen while we talk?"

"No, thank you, Father. I prefer to be by the fire with my needlework," Mehti said, knowing she did not want to miss this conversation for anything.

"That's fine. She can certainly stay," Greeley said, smiling at Mehti.

Rebecca found it hard to look in Mordecai Greeley's direction. His expression was always tight and pinched, his eyes always gawking in a way that caused her discomfort. It was no surprise to her that it was he who knocked on their door. Since the warmer spring weather had set in, she often saw him sauntering by their house in hopes of running into her. A slug in the garden could move no slower. Each time she saw him, she would redirect her course to avoid any contact. Now it was clear there was no escaping him. He intended to force the issue.

Once the four of them were seated, awkward silence filled the room, the tick of the mantel clock dominating. Finally, Gabriel began the conversation. "And to what do we owe the pleasure of your visit today, Mordecai?"

"As you know, Gabriel, I have often expressed to you my fondness for your daughter, Rebecca. I recognize that under normal conditions I should speak to you privately on these matters, but since Rebecca is now widowed, I thought perhaps she could sit in on our conversation."

Rebecca felt her spine stiffen. Mehti practiced restraint and held in a snicker.

Mordecai continued. "I observe that Rebecca is a comely woman of substance. She has some intellect about her that I admire. These are all qualities that I would agree to have complement my life, for, as you know, I am a man of substance, financially speaking. I can provide for her better than anyone in Granville, yourself included," he said smugly. "I have been patiently waiting for a suitable time of widowhood to pass before broaching the subject, but I wish to take her as my wife." Since he was not addressing Rebecca directly, at this pronouncement, he looked in her direction, but she swiftly looked away.

Silence again engulfed the room.

"That is quite an offer, Mordecai. And you have obviously thought this over carefully and taken much into consideration," Gabriel responded diplomatically. "However, I feel as a widow, Rebecca is most capable of deciding such proposals without my intervention. I think you must put the question to her directly, Mordecai."

"Very well." Mordecai stood and stepped across the room, trying to decide if he should kneel or not. He finally decided just to stand.

"Rebecca Tewkesbury, would you do me the honor of being my wife?"

"Certainly not!" Rebecca blurted out more harshly than she intended. "We have no basis for a marriage between us. You do not even know my son. I suspect you would terrify him. Not only do I have no feelings for you, something that's important to me in a marriage, but we have barely spoken to one another. We have nothing in common between us." Rebecca finally caught herself before she said another word. Mordecai's pomposity and arrogance riled her, but she did not mean to do him any harm.

"Are you quite sure of that decision?" Gabriel interjected.

"Quite." Rebecca returned to her stitching and dared not say another word.

Mordecai looked dejected as he stared incredulously at Rebecca, then back at Gabriel.

Then his eyes focused on Mehti. "Well," he said turning to Gabriel, "what about this one?"

"Excuse me?" Mehti said tilting her head in disbelief. Then she appealed to Gabriel, "Father, surely this is jest."

"I believe Mehitable is now of marrying age?" Mordecai continued, ignoring Mehti's comment.

Gabriel got to his feet and the two men stood abreast. "I beg your pardon, Mordecai. I know that loneliness can be difficult at times, as I have felt it so often since the passing of my wife,

Anna. But surely you jest at the thought of taking my fourteen-year old daughter as your wife. Good God, man. You are nearing 50."

"You are probably right, Gabriel. I am likely too much of a man for her."

Then turning to Rebecca and Mehti, he said, "I am so sorry to have disturbed your day. I saw my offers as an opportunity for either of you. Sad to say, it was an opportunity you both missed," he said, tipping his hat. "Good day, Gabriel." He turned and, without another word, let himself out the door.

Chapter 8

The following Sunday after church, Rebecca sat on the front stoop and watched Oliver who crouched to examine a grasshopper that paused in the grass. Oliver tried repeatedly to snatch the grasshopper, but it was all too quick for the inquisitive two-year-old.

"Oliver, come to Mother," Rebecca said and motioned him toward her, holding out her arms. It was a beautiful May day and, after spending the entire previous day planting the kitchen garden, Rebecca was grateful for the rest that Sunday brought. Instead of coming to his mother, Oliver began hopping every time the grasshopper hopped. Rebecca decided to let him be to burn off some of his incessant energy. She was so focused on her son, she didn't notice Frederic coming down the lane toward her.

"Bon jour, Rebecca."

Rebecca started at his greeting, then stood to receive him. He looked absolutely gallant in his full dress uniform of blue and gold. His French accent was quite thick, but his English had improved dramatically over the last few months. His warm smile never ceased to stir her.

"Bon jour, Frederic. I am so pleased you are able to join us for dinner."

"Is this Oliver?" he asked, watching the boy hop through the grass.

"Yes. As you can see, he's a very active child. I can barely keep up with him most days. Oliver, please come here. There is someone I want you to meet."

Oliver raced toward them, then stopped in his tracks and looked up at Frederic as though he were staring in awe at a beautiful sunrise.

Frederic extended his hand to Oliver. "Bon jour, juene homme. Excuse moi—Hello, young man."

Much to Rebecca's amazement, Oliver shot up both arms skyward, clasping and opening his hands toward Frederic, indicating he wished to be picked up.

Frederic looked to Rebecca for approval, and she nodded. He lifted Oliver up and the child immediately reached for Frederic's hat which was relinquished and placed on Oliver's head. The heavy festooned hat, obviously too large, covered most of Oliver's face so that only his chin was exposed, which caused some laughter. Frederic lifted it off, but held it in front of the child so he could examine it. If Rebecca didn't know better, she could have easily mistaken them for father and son, their coloring was so similar— both blond, fair skinned with matching grey eyes. She felt a lump form in her throat.

"Why don't we go inside," Rebecca said. "My family is looking forward to meeting you. But where is Claude? Was he unable to come?"

"I did not see Claude when I rose this morning. Perhaps he was detained last evening. I apologize that he is not here."

"Hopefully he will show in the course of the day," Rebecca said.

The full contingency of family came to dinner, as everyone was eager to meet Rebecca's new friend. After giving it much thought, Gabriel decided to have Hut butcher their pig, spoils from the recent privateering adventure. Ruby and Sarah roasted a portion on the fireplace spit and Mehti made baked beans that had sat in the warm coals throughout the night. The aromas set everyone's mouths watering as they sat down eagerly to enjoy the bountiful meal.

When Frederic learned the meal was courtesy of the British government, due to Hut and Jacob's valiant privateering efforts, he was interested to hear more.

"Dis past winter der not be much activity on the Sound," Hut began. "But now dat spring come, we be spendin' more and more time on da waters. Master Shaw knows we are able to go out whenever he gets word dem British ships are in de Sound."

"Nathaniel Shaw is the Connecticut Agent for the Navy. He monitors all the waterfront activity in New London, and is frequently called to Hartford to coordinate efforts," Gabriel explained as everyone passed the beans and bread. "His mansion sits right on the water on the Thames River, a perfect spot to keep apprised of all incoming and outgoing vessels. It might interest you to know, Frederic, that some twenty years ago when his father, Captain Shaw, began building his stone mansion, he hired a number of French refugees who arrived at our shores from Nova Scotia. Were it not for him, they might have starved."

"He sounds like he was a most astonishing man and a true ally to the French."

While everyone at the table was content to listen to Gabriel and Frederic in their exchange, Mehti could not contain herself from joining the conversation.

"Are you excited to be leaving Granville to join the Continental Army?" she asked.

"I will be pleased for the men when we are ordered to leave. They are restless and not accustomed to so – how do you say? – slow a place. Their idleness leads to difficulties. As for me, I have mixed feelings," Frederic said, glancing over at Rebecca, their lingering eye contact observed by all.

"Well, we are grateful for your service, Monsieur Dubois," Gabriel said.

Malcolm lay in his cradle not far from the hearth, sound asleep. But Oliver and Abigail had finished eating and were beginning to fidget in their seats, a sign to Rebecca and Rachael that the children needed to be removed. Rebecca was thankful the children had behaved as long as they had. She was about to tend to their children when a resounding knock came at the front door. Rebecca immediately thought it could be Mordecai returning for his second appeal. Or perhaps it was Claude arriving finally for dinner. But the knock displayed urgency.

Gabriel went to answer the door which could be viewed from the dining room right through to the parlor. Out of curiosity, all heads followed Gabriel's movements.

"Excuse moi," a French soldier stood facing Gabriel, his face bleak. "I seek Frederic Dubois. Can you tell me if he is here? I am sorry to interrupt, but there is an urgent matter I must discuss with him."

"Yes, of course," then turning to his guest, "Frederic, one of your men is here to see you."

Frederic immediately got up from the table and made his way to the parlor, followed by the others. The two men spoke in French while everyone stood nearby to hear what news could be so urgent. Finally, Frederic let everyone know.

"There is suspicion that Claude and another of our men have deserted. They are nowhere to be found and their horses are missing. I must go at once with a search party to find them. I apologize that I must leave so soon."

"Frederic, perhaps Jon Bear can help in your search. No one in Granville knows this part of Connecticut better than Jon Bear," Gabriel said. Jon Bear nodded in approval.

"Very well. We appreciate your assistance," Frederic said. "I thank you for your hospitality, Monsieur White. Au revoir, Madame," he said bowing toward Rebecca.

"Godspeed, Frederic, and take care."

"I will saddle Maisey," Jon Bear said, and within seconds the two men were out the door and gone.

Chapter 9

Hut's butchering job required him to travel to New London at least twice a week. After his first couple of trips, it became clear that while old man Cuthbert was gruff in nature, Hut found him to be fair in his dealings and demands. Hut thought it interesting that everyone referred to the shop owner as "old man Cuthbert," while Hut called him Mr. Cuthbert, having no idea as to his given name. On Hut's third visit to the shop, he met Ruthie Cuthbert, old man Cuthbert's wife, whom he found to be the sweetest soul.

Hut did not know the ages of the Cuthberts, but guessed they were in their 70s at the very least. What endeared him to Ruthie was that she was almost totally blind and, in spite of her difficulties, always faced each day with a lively spirit and an uplifting disposition. Ruthie didn't let her impairment keep her from being active around the house, shop or garden. In fact, old man Cuthbert relied on her heavily, probably more so than she relied on him. She often made it a point to stop by Hut's chopping block in the back of the shop to bring him cool well water, or sometimes even lemonade.

Ruthie was tiny and slight, but an energetic woman with the whitest of white hair pulled straight back and tied in a bun that rested on the nape of her neck. Her ruddy skin divulged a life of outside labor, perhaps in her gardens or along the waterfront not far from their shop. Glimpses of the beauty of her youth surfaced in her warm smile and loving nature. Her eyes appeared clouded over, but Hut could imagine they at one time bore a glint that matched her smile.

One day, to Hut's amazement, Ruthie entered the butcher shop and positioned herself in a nearby chair, a sunbeam from the only window casting light on her silvery hair as she set herself to do her needlework by feel alone. "And how is it that you have become a Tewkesbury?" she innocently asked Hut out of curiosity. Hut was in the midst of plucking chickens when he paused to consider how to share his story with Ruthie without going into too much detail.

"Me and my mammy and siblings was all slaves in Richmond, Virginia. We raised tobacco. My masta, he a drunkard dat beat on his wife until one day she lost her mind and shot him dead. We buried him out back of the house. Then the missus, she set us free. The older kids went their separate ways. The young'uns stayed behind with my mammy. I was given a letter from my misses declaring me free to go live with her folks in Albany. But I only made it as far as Pennsylvania and was 'bout half dead when Oliver Tewkesbury, Miss Becca's husband, found me, and he and Gabriel saved my life—even got me to join the army. We was at the Battle of Monmouth Courthouse—Oliver didn't make it. Miss Becca was there too. She what dey call a follower, nursing on the wounded. Anyways, before Oliver died, he give me his name. And den I met Ruby, my wife. Gabriel, he brings us all back to Connecticut. I shore am a lucky man. Miss Ruthie, does you know Miss Becca?"

"We have never met, Hut. Perhaps you could bring her with you one day."

"I shore can do dat, Miss Ruthie. Miss Becca and her sister, Mehti, dey be doing dat needlework all the time. Maybe dey come and do it wit you."

"What a splendid idea, Hut," Ruthie replied. Then, as an afterthought, she asked, "Hut, do you know what ever became of your master's wife, or your mother?"

"No, Miss Ruthie, I do not. And I may never know. I got no plans of ever going back to Richmond."

At that moment, old man Cuthbert came walking through the butcher shop in search of Ruthie.

"So, here you are," he said to Ruthie. "I've been looking hither and yon for you and here you are chatting away and keeping Hut from his work," he scolded.

"No need to be harsh, dear. Just setting for a spell."

"Well, I got that flour all ground back from the mill and you got to get out there and bag it, then get it on the shelf. Don't do no good in a fifty-pound sack."

Without another word, he wheeled around and headed back out of the room. A few noticeable moments of silence followed. Ruthie could tell her husband's temperament didn't set well with Hut, although he could never say a word.

"Don't pay him no mind, Hut," Ruthie commented as she picked up her needlework, preparing to leave. "My husband is a hardworking man who built this business with ingenuity and his own two hands. And he fusses over it so. But he's a good man. And we been together nigh these fifty-two years. I've gotten used to his ways," she said with a smile. "So please, just don't pay him no mind," she said as she felt her way out through the shop door.

Chapter 10

It had been three days since Jon Bear and Frederic left Granville, part of a posse of six riders, in search of the apparent deserter, Claude Boisvert, and Rebecca was beginning to worry.

"How far do you think they will go to bring back a deserter?" She asked Gabriel one evening. She thought the length of their absence could be attributed to the possibility they just could not find the soldier.

"Since Frederic's friend left with his horse, I would expect he traveled a good distance. Were he on foot, he would have maybe hid himself nearby and could have been easily tracked and rooted out. But on horseback, he could be as far as New York in this amount of time. I have complete confidence in Jon Bear. No one I know can track as well as he can. It would not surprise me to see them enter camp sometime tomorrow."

As Gabriel predicted, the next day just before noon, the group rode into Granville with Claude handcuffed and strapped to his horse. He sat, not stooped as one would expect, but boldly held his head high, looking straight ahead. Rebecca, who was in the garden when the posse passed by the White farmhouse, stopped to observe the procession. Frederic tipped his hat to her. Shouts echoed across the green as the soldiers began to gather, only able to guess as to the fate of their comrade.

Hearing the commotion, Gabriel and Mehti came to the side of the road and stood, watching, with Rebecca.

"What will become of him, Father?" Mehti asked.

"Claude isn't their first deserter. I understand there have been three others. But he's the first one they've captured. I suspect they will make an example of him."

"Will they tie him to a post and strap him?" Rebecca asked, shuddering at the thought.

"If he is lucky," Gabriel replied. He turned and strode back to the barn, where he had been feeding and watering Maisey and the mule, that for some unknown reason never was given a name.

"We've never had a whipping in Granville," Mehti said as she gazed after the posse now entering the encampment. "We had the last minister run out of town, him being a Tory. And then there was the burning of Arnold's effigy. But never a whipping," she said with enthusiasm. Rebecca got the impression Mehti would look forward to such an event.

"Really, Mehti," she exclaimed. "Is your life that mundane that you would look forward to seeing a man being whipped? Your thirst for adventure is too keen."

Mehti only shrugged in reply.

Rebecca was anxious to talk to Frederic, to find out how and where they were able to find Claude, but she would have to wait until he met with his commander and men. She hoped he would stop by to see her, and thought it likely she would see him sometime in the next few days.

The next morning Rebecca was feeding the chickens out by the garden, Oliver chasing after them, when Sarah joined her.

"Have you heard anything from Frederic?" Sarah asked.

"No, nothing. Has Jon Bear told you anything about Claude's capture?"

"Jon Bear said Claude intended to make his way to Quebec, but he never made it past the Connecticut River. They found him camped on this side of the river, across from Wethersfield. Jon Bear said Frederic spoke to Claude, but their conversation was in French, so he's not sure how he was convinced to return," Sarah said.

"I see Frederic as a man of honor, and I suspect he convinced Claude to return as a man or honor. I hope for his sake that they are lenient with him. Did you know they grew up together in the Alsace region of France? And they joined the service together. I wonder if Frederic will have any influence as to Claude's punishment."

The two women were surprised to see Mehti and her friend Caleb running up the lane, both out of breath.

"Have you heard? Everyone in town is talking about it," Mehti said to the women.

"Talking about what?" Rebecca asked.

"The execution! They're going to execute Claude!" Mehti said.

"Oh, Lord have mercy!" Sarah exclaimed.

"When is this to happen?" Rebecca asked.

"Mrs. Beckham told us he's to be executed by firing squad this morning," Caleb said. "It could be any moment now."

"We're heading to the encampment now, to see," Mehti chimed in. "Are you coming?" she asked, addressing both women.

"You should go," Sarah told Rebecca. "I'll take care of Oliver."

"Yes, Rebecca, you should come. Claude is Frederic's friend. You need to be there," Mehti implored her sister.

"Very well. I will go," Rebecca said. "Sarah, if you see father, please let him know what's happening and where we've gone."

Rebecca, Caleb and Mehti headed for the south part of the green, near the war office. It was a dreary day, especially for late May, and the clouds seemed to swirl in discontent, heaving a gray deathly pall over the entire town. While once the green was, in fact, quite green and lush for mowing, it was now sodden and well-trod—muddied on the rainy days.

Many of the townspeople had gotten word of the execution and stood, curious onlookers, at the edge of the green. As the three walked along the road, they could see a column of Hussars in full dress uniform parading toward the war office. Positioned next to the building was a solitary cedar pole that must have been erected before daybreak. Rebecca felt certain all 220 Hussars were in attendance. Her father was right: Lauzun's intent was to make an example of Claude, to curtail any future desertions.

Five Hussars broke rank, muskets in hand, and stepped forward when the column came to a halt about five rods from the post. Rebecca was relieved to see that Frederic was not among the executioners.

Two men brought Claude to his execution site and strapped him to the post. The gathered townsfolk began to whisper to one another with the realization that the execution they had heard about was about to happen. To Rebecca's amazement, Frederic stepped forward and approached Claude and spoke to him; but they were so distant, she could not make out his words. She felt certain there were tears running down his face. Frederic kissed Claude on both cheeks, then stood at attention and saluted him before stepping forward, covering the condemned man's head with a burlap sack. Turning on his heel, he marched away from his friend, spun and stood at attention about five rods away.

A soldier standing alongside the riflemen raised his sword and shouted in German, *"Bereit, aim, feuer!"* No translation was needed as he swung his sword downward and all five muskets fired simultaneously. Everyone covered their ears at the loud noise, which was followed by an eerie silence, smoke drifting and clouding the area. Claude's body slumped in place, blood streaming from his torso. The command was given for the men to fall back into place. The column of Hussars did an about face and began their march back across the green.

Mehti stood frozen in place after the execution. She looked around at the sound of someone retching behind her. It was Caleb, overcome at the sight of the killing.

"Caleb, my goodness. Such a thing to get sick over!" Mehti chided.

Caleb looked as pale as a sheepskin and, judging by the flush of pink rising on his cheeks, Mehti understood he felt embarrassed by his condition – even more so by her calling attention to it.

"Let me get you to our house to set a spell, perhaps get you something to drink to settle you," she offered, putting an arm around her friend's shoulder and leading him away.

Rebecca stood with her eyes closed and her hand over her mouth, unable to move or speak. Even though she had been at Valley Forge and witnessed incredible suffering, Claude's execution seemed so unnecessarily wasteful of human life. She knew Frederic would be devastated by the turn of events. She determined to wait to hear from him to allow him the time needed to absorb his loss.

As the townsfolk started to drift away, two soldiers brought a stretcher and laid it in front of Claude's body. They cut his bindings, laid his body on the stretcher and carried him away. Within minutes it was over, as if it had never occurred, and all that remained was blood-stained soil that would all too soon be washed away, leaving no trace at all.

Rebecca could not help noticing the sky cleared and the sparrows had once again begun swooping across the green, in search of bugs.

Chapter 11

The town of New London, situated at the mouth of the Thames River, had become a bastion for privateers, due to its deep harbor rivaled only by Newport and New York, and the fact that Connecticut was primarily a patriot state. So strong was Connecticut's dedication to the cause of liberty that since the beginning of the war, it never failed to provide requested provisions and men to support the effort. When some towns failed to meet their annual quota of soldiers, other towns would make up the shortfall. The privateers hailing from New London were passionate patriots who also enjoyed sharing in the bounty of their exploits.

The Thames River, its privateers and surrounding towns were protected by three forts commanding access to any ship entering or exiting the river. The most imposing of these was Fort Griswold, set upon a looming precipice on the Groton side of the river, with a commanding view – with sights on Fisher's Island and, beyond that, Long Island to the south.

When Hut first arrived in Granville in '79, the fort had been rebuilt two years earlier, a design by Col. William Ledyard, who also oversaw its reconstruction. On the same day Gabriel introduced Hut to old man Cuthbert, the two ferried across the river from New London to see the impressive structure, hiking up the steep hillside and entering the fort through an underground sally port on the southwest side. Unlike the sally port at Fort Green on Long Island that was a simple opening in the fort wall, this entrance tunneled underground for about five rods, shorn up overhead by quarried granite.

Once inside, they found the structure to be oblong shaped, with its longest side facing the Thames. The walls were made of stone and rose up twelve feet. The entire river side of the fort was surrounded by a deep trench. Above the trench were pickets that projected more than twelve feet beyond its walls. Above the pickets were embrasures with cannon platforms that consisted of one 18-pounder, seventeen 12-pounders, two nine-pounders, seven six-pounders and six four-pounders—a formidable compound.

Standing on the platform beside Gabriel, Hut was struck by the expansive view the fort afforded. "I don't see how any ship could get by dis fort," he told Gabriel as he surveyed the river and surrounding countryside.

"I agree. We could certainly give any invading Brits a good fight. Fort Trumbull is certainly less impressive but adds to the level of protection."

Almost directly across the river on the New London side, on a peninsula of land just southeast of the town, stood Fort Trumbull, named for the Connecticut governor. Its earthen breastwork extended across three sides of the fort that faced the river, leaving the backside open.

"Fort Griswold's reconstruction was started just after we entered the war, and I am proud to say I lent a hand in its building," Gabriel said. "We sledged most of this stone from adjacent fields. Several local farmers lent their oxen for the task, but it was still back-breaking work. It took us about ten months to complete.

"Fort Trumbull was built while I was away with the army. Then there's Fort Nonsense, the last to be built, which I would barely call a fort, but again, it has commanding views of the river from the top of Town Hill. It holds only six guns."

Hut looked out across the river and to the hillside above Fort Trumbull, the area of town Gabriel had pointed out known as Town Hill. Fort Nonsense was a discernable earthwork construction, but not as formidable as the fort he stood in now. "It gives me a feeling of safety, these forts," he said.

"That's why I wanted to bring you up here. I know you've viewed the forts from the *Josephine,* but coming here gives an entirely broader perspective. And I feel the same as you do. With these forts manned by a strong militia, the British would find a great difficulty staging an offense against New London and Groton."

"I agree."

64

"Now Col. Ledyard oversees all three forts. You will find no greater patriot among us than Col. William Ledyard, except perhaps Nathanial Shaw, Jr., and his wife, Lucretia. You can see their home from here, as well. It's that three-story granite structure just beyond the wharves on Bank Street," Gabriel said as he pointed across the river to the large stone home not far from the water's edge. "Shaw and his wife have taken countless sailors and soldiers into their home in their hour of need. Lucretia nursed them, regardless of the risk to her own health. She is an amazing woman."

The two men stood, again taking in the view of the town, river and Long Island Sound.

"The wind is picking up," Gabriel noted. "Maybe a storm is brewing. We should head back across the river and get home before dark."

The two men exited through the sally port and made their way back down the hillside to the ferry slip.

Chapter 12

Since Claude's execution, Rebecca vowed she would not go to the encampment to seek out Frederic – because she wanted to respect his time of mourning. What helped her keep her promise was her twice-weekly trips to New London accompanying Hut, often with Mehti and Caleb in tow.

And then there was Ruthie Cuthbert.

"I would like you to meet her. You will like dis woman," Hut exclaimed. "And she will welcome your company. Jus come once and meet her," he implored. Over the past two weeks, Hut had harnessed the horse and donkey to the wagon and the four made their way to New London, leaving Granville in the early morning hours.

When Rebecca first met Ruthie, she felt a kindred connection that was totally unexpected. Hut's intuition had been correct. The two women sat down to their needlework and chatted amicably, their flow of words effortless. Something about Ruthie reminded Rebecca of her mother, although she could not specifically understand what it was about the woman that brought her that level of comfort. Ruthie possessed a strength of character lurking beneath her unassuming nature. She amazed Rebecca with her ability at needlework, despite her lack of vision. All stitches were done by feel and the palette of colors was mapped in her mind. She could see what she was creating in her imagination. And Rebecca helped her only by handing her the color threads she requested.

"I think a pale yellow will go well on the outside of these flowers, Rebecca. Would you hand me a strand, dear?" she asked. To Rebecca's amazement, Ruthie successfully threaded her needles by feel.

Generally an afternoon visit would be around two or three hours, at which time Ruthie would have to return to manning the store and preparing the afternoon meal. During that time, Hut butchered away in the shop, and Mehti and Caleb roamed and explored the wharves that were a bustle of activity, so much more exciting than docile life in Granville.

Mehti in particular loved being on the waterfront. The two strolled up and down Bank Street, which ran along the banks of the Thames River, and ventured out on every wharf to observe each ship's activities. Where were the ships from? What cargo were they carrying? Where were they traveling next? Mehti often packed a lunch and they'd find some crates on one of the piers and sit by the water to consume their meal as they watched the activities of the seamen. There was something about being by the water that made Mehti feel more alive. The movement of the water, the fresh breezes and the hustle of activity were rejuvenating.

"I'd like to go see Captain Treadwell today, Mehti," Caleb said, breaking Mehti's trance as she stared out at the river.

"Whatever for?"

"I've been talking to Hut. He says Treadwell might welcome another seaman on their privateering voyages." He straightened his spine and held up his chest as if to look more the part of a seaman.

"Surely you jest, Caleb," Mehti chided. "You're way too young to be engaged in such activity."

"That's simply not true, Mehti. How old was Jacob when he went off and joined the army? Wasn't he fifteen?"

"That was different. He went with Oliver and our neighbor. They took care of one another."

"And so will Hut, Jacob and I. We'll take care of each other, as well. Besides, it's not like I'm joining the army and leaving home. Just going out on some voyages when called upon."

Mehti put down her cornbread. "What is this all about, Caleb? Are you feeling as though you now have to prove yourself a man after I made fun of your getting sick at the execution? Privateering is risky and nothing to take lightly. You could be seriously injured, captured or killed. And I will point out to you that Jacob came back missing part of an arm, and our neighbor, Jesse, did not come back at all."

"And would you care if I were injured, captured or killed?" he asked.

"You are incorrigible!" Mehti exclaimed, feeling trapped by her own words. Staring out at the water again, she could not help glancing over at Caleb, his jaw firm. The sun highlighted his blond, wind-blown curls. In spite of her protests, he inexplicably appeared to her now as more handsome than ever.

The two finished their meal and headed toward the *Josephine*. Along the way, they passed by Mr. Shaw and his wife, out for an afternoon stroll. It was Shaw who oversaw all the privateering efforts out of the port.

"Good day, Mehitable," he said tipping his tri-corner.

"Good day, Captain," Mehti responded with a slight curtsey. "And good day to you, Mrs. Shaw. Mr. Shaw, I am so pleased to run into you. I still have your spyglass and hope I may keep it in service. My friend Caleb and I keep a watch out from General Neck regularly. But if you need it back, please just let me know."

"Quite all right. You keep to that task and keep us informed. All hands are needed and we appreciate your help."

"I will, sir." And with that brief encounter, they parted their ways.

It took no time at all for Caleb to track down Captain Treadwell on his sloop. Mehti said nothing as the two men discussed Caleb's possible role as part of the crew. While Hut acted as first mate, it was decided Caleb would assist as needed, and that was all he could ask for.

"You look strong enough to me," Treadwell commented as he took hold of Caleb's upper arm. While Caleb was tall, he was quite lanky and Mehti had difficulty picturing this gentle soul with a saber in one hand and a pistol in the other. She stood by warily as the two shook on their agreement.

The ride back home was fairly quiet, everyone deep in thought. Rebecca was beginning to feel she should no longer keep her distance from Frederic. Surely enough time had passed for him to have begun to heal from his loss. Once she set her resolve, she was determined to seek him out – and wasted no time once they returned to Granville. As soon as they arrived home, she woke Oliver from his afternoon nap.

"Oliver, come with Mother. We are going to visit Frederic. Would you like that?"

Oliver nodded as he rubbed the sleep out of his eyes.

The two of them walked down the lane and entered the encampment. There seemed to be an unusual amount of activity as soldiers scurried about. Rumor was the Hussars would be leaving within the next few weeks, heading for Philipsburg, New York to join Washington and his troops. The thought of Frederic's leaving reminded Rebecca of Oliver's leaving in '76. She pushed the thought out of her mind, lest it cause her unwanted anxiety. Just the thought of Frederic leaving caused enough distress.

When they finally reached Frederic's cabin, he was nowhere in sight. Rebecca poked her head in the cabin and noted it was vacant, except for one soldier who sat, brush in hand, polishing his boots. When he caught her gaze, he immediately stood.

"Excuse me, but I am looking for Frederic. I am his English tutor."

"Oh, yes, Madame. He was here not too long ago. We have been so busy with preparations to leave. Many of the men are using these last days to write home. I believe you can find Frederic out at the dinner tables under the trees."

The soldier pointed in the direction on the north side of the green. "I see that his ink pot and pen are missing. He wanted to write to his wife and this might be his last opportunity. One never knows what battle might bring to us."

Rebecca felt the blood drain from her face. She momentarily felt faint and only realized she was squeezing Oliver's hand too tightly when he began to squirm.

"Yes, of course," she stammered. "Thank you for your help."

"Shall I tell him you were looking for him?"

"No, no, that will not be necessary," she stuttered. "I will seek him out at a more opportune time, so as not to disturb him."

Rebecca spun on her heel and made a hasty retreat. She felt in a crazed state of shock and dared not look but straight ahead, lest her eyes fall upon Frederic. Humiliation overcame her and she fought back tears, determined to get home as quickly as possible. Once there, she scurried through the sitting room and headed upstairs.

"Rebecca?" her father called out from the kitchen when he heard someone rushing through the house.

"Father, I wish to not be disturbed," she called back as she lifted Oliver onto her hip and headed up the stairs. Once inside her room, she sat on her bed, cradling Oliver in her lap, and began to cry.

Chapter 13

Frederic stood on the front stoop of the White household. So many weeks had passed since he had last seen Rebecca, he thought perhaps she had been ill. While it was true he had not sought her out, he wondered why she had made no attempt to contact him. Admittedly, since Claude's death, he had found it difficult to be sociable with anyone and kept mostly to himself, or spent most of his time in riding maneuvers. He barely took notice as one day seamlessly passed into another. At some point he finally realized the passage of time. Thoughts of Rebecca flooded back into his consciousness and he slowly acknowledged he missed her terribly. As his numbness wore off like a lifting fog, what he barely noticed before became evident: The entire camp was deeply engaged in preparations to leave Granville and he had little time remaining to make preparations.

He hesitated, then tentatively knocked on the door. There was no response. Glancing around the property, he saw no one. It seemed unusual to him that just prior to the dinner hour, no one would be available to answer the door. Perhaps Rebecca was seriously ill. He knocked harder, using his fist, when the door flew open. Gabriel White stood before him.

"Gabriel, I hope I didn't disturb you."

"Not at all."

"I wonder if I might speak with Rebecca. We prepare to leave shortly and I haven't had an opportunity to see or speak with her for some time. I hope very much to see her before we begin our travels."

Gabriel hesitated. He had no idea why Rebecca had asked not to receive Frederic should he come visiting, but he knew he should honor her request.

"I am afraid she is not available."

"Has she been ill?"

Gabriel was uncertain how to respond. "No, she is quite well. Just not available at the moment."

"May I return tomorrow?" Frederic asked in earnest.

"If it pleases you, but I cannot assure she will be available at that time either." Gabriel cleared his throat and stared at the floor, uncertain of what might have transpired between Rebecca and Frederic, two people he observed could not keep their eyes off each other at his dinner table just a few weeks earlier.

"I see," Frederic responded as he glanced up at a second-story window and saw the curtains abruptly close. "I don't know what to say. We leave in two days. If it is not too much to ask, would you please be sure to let her know that I came to see her?"

"Certainly," Gabriel said, feeling sympathy for the young soldier about to go off to fight for the colonies. He was puzzled by what had caused Rebecca to rebuff Frederic, but respected her wishes.

Frederic left as Gabriel slowly closed the door, but glanced back several times at the second-floor window in hopes he would catch a glimpse of Rebecca; but the curtains remained closed.

The next day, Frederic returned to the White farmhouse. It was his last opportunity to see Rebecca, as the Hussars were scheduled to leave at first light. This time Mehti answered the door.

"Why, Frederic," Mehti exclaimed, happy to see him. "Where have you been? I haven't seen you in so long. It is so good of you to stop by. I was afraid I wouldn't get a chance to see you before you left."

"Mehti, it is so good to see you as well. Is Rebecca home by any chance?"

"No, this is her day to go into New London with Hut. We expect her at the dinner hour. May I give her a message?"

"Mehti, it seems she may be avoiding me and I am unsure why. Do you have any idea what may be plaguing her so much that she will not see me?"

"Truly, I have no idea, Frederic. But when she returns home, I will question her, you may be sure. Something is amiss. I can assure you that Rebecca has shown nothing but the greatest appreciation for your company."

"Thank you, Mehti. I appreciate your assistance in this instance. I will wait to hear from you," Frederic said as he tipped his hat and left.

That afternoon, thick clouds obscured the skies, followed by downpours that hampered not only the soldiers' preparations, but Rebecca and Hut's return home. Mehti paced the sitting-room floor, stopping occasionally to stoke the fire that continued to burn, even on this, the eve of the first day of summer. The room was sweltering and Mehti finally decided to leave open the front door, to allow some fresh, albeit moist, air to make its way into the house.

A deafening lightning crack unnerved her as the rains pummeled the green, flattening the hay on the south green that should have been mowed the prior day. She thought about the conditions of the roads and wondered whether Hut and Rebecca would consider staying over in Norwich, rather than make the entire trip home. Rebecca had never spent an entire night away from Oliver, who was being cared for by his Aunt Sarah and Uncle Jon Bear.

To pass the time and provide relief from worry, she allowed her thoughts to wander, wondering what would become of the cabins being left behind by the exiting soldiers. Perhaps they would sit and rot; but more likely the townspeople would dismantle them and save the logs for firewood or split it and use it as fencing. As afternoon turned into evening and then night, she felt certain Rebecca and Hut would not return home until the morrow, and she retired to bed.

The rooster's crow awoke Mehti the moment a hint of pre-dawn light reached the edge of the town green. She leapt out of bed, raced down stairs to the front door and stood on the stoop in only her nightdress. The night's heavy rains had abated, leaving wafts of steam languishing above the green. The damp air carried a musty aroma of earth and smoke.

Glancing toward the barn, Mehti could see the wagon had been returned, but left out in haste, while Maisey had apparently been led to her stall. *So, Rebecca returned in the middle of the night, after all.* Mehti hurried back into the house and up to Rebecca's bedchamber. She tapped lightly on the door and called to her sister.

"Rebecca, may I come in?"

Mehti heard a low groan and took it as a sign to enter, which she did. She gently shook her sister's arm to waken her.

"Becca, please wake up. I realize you must be tired, but there is something we must discuss and time is of the essence. Please Becca, I promised Frederic."

"Frederic?" Rebecca responded, not wanting to acknowledge the stir his name caused within her.

"Yes, Becca. The Hussars are leaving this morning and he's been here looking for you, hoping to see you before he leaves. Has he offended you in some way? I am confused that you have not mentioned his name once in the last few weeks. Tell me, how has he sullied your feelings for him?"

Rebecca sat up in bed and rubbed the sleep out of her eyes. "It's no use, Mehti. He is not the man I thought he was."

"What nonsense do you speak?" Mehti almost scolded, then caught herself. "He is as good a gentleman as any woman could have on her arm."

"I have been ashamed to tell anyone, Mehti—ashamed of my foolhardiness. Father doesn't even know. I have by happenstance discovered that Frederic is married, Mehti," she said as her eyes began to well up with tears. She immediately shook them off, focusing her eyes to the ceiling to help gain her composure.

"Surely not!" Mehti exclaimed. "Who told you such a lie?"

"I sought him out at his cabin a couple of weeks after Claude's death. I spoke with his cabin mate, who told me he was off writing a letter to his wife. I have felt too humiliated to tell anyone."

Mehti could not believe what she was hearing. She stood and began pacing the room. "This cannot be. There must be some misunderstanding. Frederic is a man of honor. I would swear to it."

78

She stopped abruptly and wheeled around to face her sister. "Did you ask for Frederic Dubois?"

Rebecca thought for a moment, trying to recall the exact conversation. "I believe I did not, but what difference does that make?"

"I know the men in that cabin. I have cooked and sewn for them all at one time or another. Rebecca, there is an older soldier there named Johann Frederic. He sometimes goes by the name of Frederic. I think the two have been confused. It is possible, Becca," Mehti said emphatically. "The men are preparing to leave. You must go and find Frederic. You must find out the truth," she begged.

"Do you really think it's possible this is just a confusion?" Rebecca said, a look of urgency suddenly taking command of her facial expression, her every move, as she leapt from the bed, careful not to wake Oliver who slept peacefully by her side. "I must go at once. What if it's too late? Can you watch Oliver for me? Do you think they've left already?" she prattled as she grabbed her day dress and hurriedly slipped it on. "My hair! It is all disheveled. Quick, hand me my bonnet," she said as she pulled her hair back, donned her bonnet and tied it in place. She bent over the wash bowl and splashed water on her face, dried it off and turned to face Mehti. "Will this do?"

"It will have to," Mehti replied as she spun her sister around and practically shoved her out the bedroom door.

There was no need to grab her shawl on this first day of summer as the morning temperatures even at this early hour were quite warm. The green was eerily silent, devoid of the usual clamor of morning troop activities.

They've already left! Panic caused Rebecca's heart to palpitate. Grabbing her skirts, she moved as swiftly as her feet would go through the quagmire left from the previous night's downpours. She stopped on the south edge of the green. Looking west down the road toward Colchester, she spied the rear column of mounted Hussars sauntering, two abreast, some 40 rods away, making their final exit from Granville. Her mind reeled, not knowing whether she should try to catch up with them. Was it too late? Should she even try? What would Frederic think of her? And his fellow Hussars, what would they make of her? In an instant, she made her decision, again lifted her now mud-soaked skirts and headed at a quick pace toward the column of riders.

Trying to outpace even a slow-moving column on horseback was no easy feat, especially given the road conditions. Rebecca struggled to maintain her balance and not fall by the roadside or slip in the mud. She dodged deep ruts along the way, which slowed her down, but she could clearly see she was gaining ground.

Finally, after about thirty minutes, she caught up to the caravan and gained the attention of the last soldier.

"Excuse me," she panted was she trod alongside the soldier. "I seek Frederic Dubois. Do you know where he is in the column?" The soldier responded that Frederic was about halfway up.

"Thank you." Rebecca again grabbed her skirts and, with determination, raced along the flanks of the column, again being cautious that the slipperiness of the road edge did not cause her to lose her footing. Heads turned as she passed each pair of riders. Within ten minutes she felt certain she had located Frederic, his blond locks protruding from beneath his hat.

Frederic had left Granville down hearted that Rebecca had not tried to contact him. He had done all he could and just had to accept that he had somehow lost her affections. So it was a most pleasant surprise when he felt a tug at his stirrups and looked down to see Rebecca's sweat-soaked face looking up at him. He immediately pulled his horse out of the column and dismounted, letting the other riders move on without him.

Frederic clutched Rebecca by both shoulders and looked down into her eyes, his chest bursting with joy to see her.

"Frederic, I am here to ask you but one question," Rebecca said, trying to contain herself. "Are you married?"

"Married! What on earth gave you such an idea? My heart belongs to no one but you, Rebecca. You must know that." He took her into his arms as she began to weep.

"I'm so sorry," Rebecca sobbed. "I thought you were the Frederic in your cabin I was told was writing a letter to his wife." Then pulling away and wiping her eyes she added, "I am so pleased that I caught up with you in time. Will you write to me?"

"You know I will. But will you wait for me?"

Too choked up for words, Rebecca simply nodded. Lifting her chin, Frederic pressed his lips against hers with a gentle, enduring kiss that was their first; and the world, and the soldiers, and any worry about impending battles, drifted away like leaves on a breezy day.

A piercing whistle from one of Frederic's comrades broke their embrace.

"Please wait for me, Rebecca," Frederic whispered. Then he mounted his horse and sped to catch up to his column, leaving Rebecca standing by the side of the road.

Chapter 14

Three weeks had passed since Frederic had left Rebecca, her mind in a whirl, her heart in her throat; and she still had not received word from him. She had heard that the Hussars had met up with the Continental Army in New York and together they headed south for Philadelphia. Rebecca would often stop by the White Horse Tavern, hoping to find out about troop movements. Or she would frequent the waterfront in New London, with Mehti and Caleb accompanying her along the wharfs, where they quizzed the sailors for new information.

Since becoming a hand on the *Josephine,* Caleb had ventured out twice in search of British vessels to commandeer, but their efforts proved fruitless. Their privateering excursions generally lasted no more than two days as they steered the *Josephine* out beyond Montauk Point into the Atlantic, or sailed east down the north side of Long Island, always on the lookout for British vessels—particularly merchant vessels short on cannon with little means of protecting themselves.

"Maybe you should count your blessings," Captain Treadwell told Caleb as he ruffled his hair and gave him a slight shove. Caleb had been pouty, itching for an encounter. "Privateering can be dangerous work and so far you've lived to tell about two voyages. That may not always be the case," Treadwell observed.

Every time Caleb went out to sea, Mehti found herself down at the waterfront, pacing the wharf, waiting impatiently, worried beyond what even she could comprehend. But on this day in July, Hut, Mehti, Caleb and Rebecca decided to stroll along the river after spending the afternoon with Ruthie Cuthbert. While Hut butchered two pigs, the other three helped Ruthie stock shelves in the store. The Cuthberts had become like second family to the Whites and Tewkesburys. Even old man Cuthbert, with his bristling ways, had managed to become endearing to them.

The day was as bright and sunny as any summer's day, and the stench emanating from the docks were as nauseating as ever, given the heat of the day. Accustomed to the odors, the four headed north along the waterfront, glimpsing the stores of goods being unloaded—sugar and rum from the islands, wood and salt cod from the north. All of a sudden, a commotion of excitement traveled up and down the docks like a rolling wave. At first, Rebecca had no idea what was happening. Looking around to see the cause of so much excitement, she noticed all heads turned toward the mouth of the Thames River as people pointed, gasped, shaded their eyes for a better view and then began to cheer.

The four looked south to see two ships tacking up the Thames. Caleb immediately recognized the trailing ship as the privateer, *Minerva* that often docked alongside the *Josephine*. Preceding the *Minerva* was what appeared to be a captured British vessel, its colors lowered in submission.

The excitement along the shore mounted as men, women and children raced along the waterfront, anxious to see where the vessels would dock. Word had traveled fast as the bells of the Episcopal church began to ring out, a message of conquering jubilation. As the British vessel neared the docks, below and to the right of the figurehead could clearly be seen emblazoned in gold, *HMS Hannah.* The figurehead displayed a bosomy blonde maiden Rebecca assumed captured the image of ship's namesake.

The wharf became crowded as onlookers craned their necks in anticipation of news from crew members. Caleb ran headlong into the mass of people, eager to be one of the first to hear of the *Minerva*'s exploits.

"Caleb!" Mehti called after him. "What foolishness and folly is this?" she said to Rebecca who waited patiently with Mehti at the back of the crowd. "He is like an impetuous child anxious to know if his father has brought him a confection."

"He seeks the glory of such a prize capture for himself," Rebecca responded.

"I swear he will get himself killed in a privateering venture one of these days," Mehti exclaimed, her expression exposing concern more than anger.

From several yards away, Caleb turned and waved to Mehti through the crowd, his face lit up, like a boy having caught his first fish. After both ships were finally anchored and tethered, the gangplank was lowered and people began backing away to allow the crew to disembark. Several privateers from the *Minerva* made their way down the plank and through the crowd. As Mehti looked over both ships, it was clear they were similar in size and cannon power. She felt certain the *HMS Hannah* was not an easy capture. But it was unclear whether there were any American causalities, as she saw no bodies being removed. She could see that Caleb had gained the ear of one of *Minerva*'s seamen and was deeply engaged in conversation. Finally, he made his way back through the crowd to share his information.

"For two turns of the hourglass they fought," he told Mehti, Rebecca and Hut, excitedly. "Isn't she magnificent?" he added, gesturing to the *Hannah*. "Sixteen six-pounders and we captured her," he bragged as if he'd been a part of the haul. "They've been nine weeks at sea out of London. And here's the best news of all! This ship is General Clinton's personal property, and they're saying the cargo may be the largest of any privateering exploit!" He was breathing heavily in his excitement as he relayed information of the capture.

"Were there any causalities?" Mehti asked.

"Oh, I forgot to ask," Caleb responded nonchalantly.

Hut was taking in all this information when he spoke up. "I tink maybe I should stay in New London for some time. Dis here boat will need to be unloaded and that will take some time—days, maybe weeks. But there be money to be made. I tink all dis cargo be stored in the warehouses on Bradley Street. I'll talk to the first mate on the *Minerva* and see what de captain plan to do."

No sooner had Hut commented than Captain Dudley Saltonstall made his way down the gangplank and along the wharf. Mehti thought he had a somewhat arrogant look about him, striding with his nose in the air. She took an immediate dislike to the man, in part because she had heard he dealt in slave trade.

News of the capture of the *HMS Hannah* had spread quickly throughout the colonies; Caleb, Rebecca and Mehti did their share by informing anyone they met along the road back to Granville on a hot August evening.

Chapter 15

Mordecai Greeley decided to keep to himself in the weeks following the humiliation he suffered at the rejection and insults afforded him by the White family—particularly Gabriel White. Twice Mordecai passed Gabriel on the road and stared staunchly ahead, silent, when Gabriel tipped his hat with a "Mornin' to you, Mordecai." *The nerve of that man. His insensitivity is astounding.* For White to think they could actually be on sociable terms after the treatment he had received infuriated Mordecai. The more time went by, the angrier he became.

He sat in his substantial parlor, glancing down at the plush brocade of his upholstered chair. It ceased to bring him the sense of comfort it once did. What good did it do him to own such things if they did not serve their intended purpose--to provide an extravagant household for a woman worthy of his bed? It occurred to him that perhaps he had overestimated Rebecca Tewkesbury's worthiness. Unknown to her, for days after her unfathomable refusal of his proposal, he had secretly tracked her every move, in hopes he could find her alone and appeal to her better senses without her father's interference. He even stood in the shadows, unseen at night, just outside her bedroom window, hoping to catch a glimpse of her. And then, how disgusted he felt to see her chasing after that useless Frenchman on the morning the Hussars departed. Did she have no pride?

As was often the case, his feelings wavered from disgust to yearning, which frustrated him even more. Perhaps he could write her. No, that would not do. Someone could intercept his correspondence and find him out. A sense of torment captured him, so frustrating was his constant state of vacillation. One moment he was loathful of the woman for her weakness and rejection – at times even visualizing his hands around her throat, shaking her violently in an attempt to let her know the seriousness of her deeds. Then, in a quick reversal, his thoughts wandered to what it would be like to hold her, to caress her, to kiss her with the passion that churned in him whenever he risked looking into her eyes.

Pacing his parlor, he realized he was obsessed. In sheer anguish, he pulled at his hair, then sat again, trying to calm his wits. But the feeling of torment was too great to overcome and he buried his head in his hands. He realized he was sweating and was becoming short of breath. He gripped the arms of his chair then held his trembling, bony hands out in front of him. He clasped them together, wringing them to stop the shaking. Confused by these symptoms, something occurred to him that had not before. He might very well be possessed. What kind of person would cause a man to feel so possessed that he is unable to rid his mind of such thoughts? What kind of woman would cause a man to break out into a sweat and question his own sanity? He was not possessed, but bewitched. It was the most logical answer. There was an evilness about her, he was sure of it now.

Mordecai jumped up from his seat, rejuvenated by this new revelation. His mind began to cascade through a rapid series of thoughts, wondering about his every contact with Rebecca. He searched his memory in an attempt to identify when exactly she might have cast this spell on him. He became giddy with relief to finally understand the cause of his torment, his madness. There was no other explanation. His mind was suddenly overtaken by a clarity of purpose. He vigorously rubbed his hands together in speculation of a solution. And within just a few moments, he knew exactly what he must do.

Chapter 16

Finally, it came. Rebecca turned the letter over and over in her hands, ran her fingertips across the wax seal, and took a deep breath before opening Frederic's letter. It had been almost six weeks since the Hussars evacuated Granville and the relative peace and quiet of their little community made it seem eerily like a ghost town. Rebecca understood the relief some of her neighbors expressed when the French left. But she had trouble feeling even a modicum of joy over their parting when all she could feel was a deep sense of loss.

The beginning of harvest time was upon them and, as she sat on their front stoop, staring down at the letter, she wondered if she should get back to the fields and save the letter to read in the evening, but she could not contain herself. Glancing up, she could see that Oliver was quite content with drawing lines in the dirt, stick in hand. She slipped her finger beneath the wax seal and opened the letter.

July 20, 1781

My sweet Rebecca:

After three weeks marching through Connecticut, we met with Washington and the American army at a place called Dobbs Ferry in New York. We Hussars are positioned fifteen miles south to guard from that location.

It was startling to see your army, so many boys, and so poorly dressed it saddened me. We do what we can to help them. All the French officers were anxious to glimpse Washington as he has become a legend among them. Some of them asked for his signature on paper, proof they have met him.

Everywhere we march we see the devastation of war—houses burned or abandoned, fields fallow. It is sad to see such beautiful country so badly scarred by war. The army now turns south and we will soon be marching through Philadelphia. I am told it is a beautiful city and we will traverse it in parade.

My thoughts of you and our last encounter sustain me. I do not know, my sweet, what the outcome of this war will be. We are confident our combined forces under the strong leadership of Washington and Rochambeau will be victorious. And when that happens, I will be at liberty to return to you. I must go now. Please think of me, as I think of you daily. Please remember me. Know that I am well.

If I may be so bold, my love to you,

Frederic

Rebecca took a deep breath and clutched the letter to her chest. She felt simultaneously full of joy and fear—joy, knowing she remained in the thoughts of Frederic as he had remained in hers, but in fear for his safety.

A flurry of activity by the barn door caught her attention. Hut had Maisey by the reins and was leading her out of the barn while Jacob scurried toward the house.

"We just got word the *Josephine*'s heading out tonight. I sent Mehti to fetch Caleb," Jacob said as he rushed past Rebecca and headed into the house. "Got to take a few provisions. I have no idea how long this trip will take."

"But the harvest!" Rebecca exclaimed.

"For now the harvest will be left to you, Dad and Jon Bear. I'm sure Sarah and Rachael will help, as well. The root crops can wait. I told Dad you should all focus on bringing in the early corn."

Rebecca noted that as her father became less and less physically able to manage the farm, Jacob took on a larger role, not only with the work demands, but with making decisions on what would be done and how it would be done. Jon Bear had always deferred to Gabriel, but now often sought out Jacob for direction on farm chores. It occurred to Rebecca this subtle shift of authority had occurred naturally, without a word being spoken.

Rebecca shook her head in dismay at the thought of the *Josephine* going out on a mission again. After spending the entire previous week in New London working for the Cuthberts, as well as helping to unload the captured *Hannah,* Hut had just returned the day before to assist with the harvest and now he would be off again.

"Will this war never end?" she exclaimed in exasperation.

Looking up the lane, Rebecca could see Caleb, with Mehti behind him, riding horseback toward the house. She assumed the three men would make the trip to New London by horse, given that the mule and wagon would be needed for the harvest. Caleb assisted Mehti off his horse then waited for Hut and Jacob to join him for the ride to New London. She guessed a night time raid on some unsuspecting British vessel would take place this very night.

Rebecca watched Mehti's trembling hands slip away from Caleb's as they said their goodbyes. It was rare to see Mehti get emotional about anything. But the scene of the two of them brought thoughts flooding back to her of Frederic's leaving, and it occurred to her that she and her sister were suffering the same kind of separations. The two sisters sat on the stoop and watched Hut, Jacob and Caleb ride off, knives and pistols packed along with their provisions.

"Well, we should probably get back to the field," Mehti said. A look of stern composure now blanketed her face.

"Let me just get Oliver," Rebecca said as she went to scoop up her son. Looking up the lane, she could see Mordecai Greeley about to pass by their house some two rods away. She lifted up Oliver and was about to wave to Mordecai when she noticed a scowl on his face that sent shivers down her body. His face looked drawn, but his stare was piercing. Then he did a peculiar thing. He lifted his cane and made the sign of a cross with his forearm as he passed by her.

What a peculiar man! Rebecca lifted her skirts and nervously headed toward the front door. She turned and looked back in Mordecai's direction before entering the house. He stood like a statue, his makeshift cross raised even higher, his scowl hardened on his face.

Chapter 17

It was just about dusk when the trio of privateers left their horses with the Cuthberts and headed for the wharf, where approximately twenty-five enthusiastic Sons of Liberty had gathered. Munitions and crew were being transported by whale boat to the *Josephine*, anchored off shore in the Thames.

"We got word this morning from a rider out of Narragansett that a British schooner was sighted heading east toward the Sound, heavily laden, given its deep water line," one sailor told them as they made their way out onto the wharf. "It could be a good haul and easier to catch if it's weighed down."

Caleb could barely contain his excitement. The three men smiled broadly at the prospect of another successful capture.

The winds were slight along the Thames, but once out in the Sound, there was hope the winds would be more favorable. New London had always been a safe haven—a bastion of patriots. Unlike other river towns in northern parts of New England, the *Josephine* attracted no enemy musket fire from Tories on land as it exited the Thames, passed the western tip of Fisher's Island and entered Long Island Sound. The evening visibility remained, as a rising sliver moon slightly illuminated the Sound, shimmering along wave tops. As expected, once out on the Sound, the winds picked up, the sails billowed and the *Josephine* sliced through the chop.

In the hustle of ship preparation, Captain Treadwell took a moment to speak with Caleb as they passed each other on deck.

"Stay close to Hut," Treadwell commanded, patting Caleb on the shoulder. Then, moving as swiftly as a plague, he crossed the deck, shouting commands along the way. "Keep those lamp lights dim!" he yelled to no one in particular. Caleb could feel the high energy of the other men, wrought of both anxiety and anticipation. With the sails set, he stopped for a moment to search for a horizon—some definition between ocean and sky—but there was none. In a brief moment of inactivity, he could feel his heart pounding in his chest. He took a deep breath to calm his nerves and rested his hand on the cutlass strung around his waist. *Could I actually kill another human being?* he wondered. *Yes,* he surmised immediately, *if I had to protect myself.* And in doing so, he would prove to Mehti he was a man—a brave man.

Caleb let his mind wander to a scene of victory and jubilation upon the return of the *Josephine*, escorting her captive British ship up the Thames. Mehti would be waiting on the docks for him, eager to render up a hero's embrace. He shook his head to dismiss the image and again focused on the murky waters of the Sound.

Captain Treadwell sat below deck, posting entries into the ship's log, when the call was yelled out from a lookout strapped to the main mast at the yard. "Ship sighted, eleven o'clock, port!"

All eyes strained to view the ship, barely visible, less than a quarter mile southwest of their position. Its speed could not be discerned, but Treadwell ordered full sail and men scurried about the deck to unfurl all sails. Caleb made his way to the bow sprint to set the jib, a job most sailors preferred not to tackle, lest they lose their grip and fall into the seas. He executed the task like a well-trained sailor. He had learned to steer clear of the billowing jib once the wind grabbed it.

With the British ship coming more fully into view, all eyes strained to keep its enlarging silhouette in focus. Hut noted the weather was perfect for a capture and the British vessel's sluggish movement guaranteed a boarding. Whether or not a capture would occur was another matter. All hands were on deck, including Captain Treadwell, as the twenty-five or so crewmen gathered, awaiting their fate.

Captain Treadwell knew the importance of timing the trim of the sails to slow the *Josephine*, enabling her to come aside the British vessel. It would be a grievous error if the *Josephine*'s forward momentum forced her to pass by the British, causing his ship to take on cannon fire, and then need to turn and tack back to engage the ship. He also knew the men were counting on his knowledge of the sea and the ship to make the right decision at the right time. Trimming the sails too early would mean they'd have to set sail again, and that would give the British enough opportunity to turn about and initiate aggression. Treadwell liked being in command of events to his and his crew's favor.

The men all stood, their anxious faces were etched with moonlight as they turned from the British ship to their captain's face, awaiting his command. The darkness played tricks on a man's vision and distance was harder to discern than in the light of day.

Hut wondered if the British ship even knew the *Josephine* was on its heels when the ship suddenly came about at an angle and fired a warning cannon blast in their direction, a shot that fell short by a hundred yards.

"We won't be intimidated," one of the men yelled as he held his musket over his head in a gesture of defiance.

"Hoozah," the men yelled, the adrenaline in their veins knowing no bounds.

"Quiet!" Treadwell yelled above their voices. "Await your commands!" He too could feel that same adrenaline and, while he appreciated his crew's enthusiasm, their hearing his commands was of the utmost importance. The men watched and waited, some unknowingly swaying from side to side in eager anticipation of the ensuing battle. Then it came.

"Trim the sails!" Treadwell bellowed, and several men, including Hut, scampered up the shrouds to the yardarms and swiftly gathered up the sails, slowing the *Josephine,* then returned to the main deck. Another cannon shot barely missed the privateer now that they were within range. With the British vessel broadside to the *Josephine,* and her sails trimmed, Treadwell thought it impossible to come alongside, as he had planned. His only course of action was to ram them with the bow.

"Man the cannon!"

Men immediately rallied to their gunner stations and fired off several rounds of deafening cannon blasts, but none hit their mark. Coming up swiftly on the British ship to within twenty yards, the pacing Captain yelled, "Grenades!" and the men began lobbing the few grenades they had on board. Unlike the cannon failures, the grenades found the deck of the enemy; but some were hastily gathered and thrown overboard. One unfortunate sailor was unsuccessful in his release of the ordnance, which blew up in his hand.

"Muskets!" Treadwell ordered as soon as they were within range. The British returned fire. It was clear to Treadwell his ship was moving too swiftly and could very well pass by their enemy. He grabbed the wheel from a crewman and steered the *Josephine* into the starboard bow of the enemy ship, so as not to pass it by. The two ships groaned as they collided, wood splintering wood, then veered and listed, the *Josephine*'s bow sprint breaking away.

"Grappling hooks!" the captain yelled above the noise of musket fire. Uncertain anyone could hear or even see him through the gun smoke, he grabbed two hooks and launched them toward the enemy's deck, then secured them to the bulwarks, the two ships now moving as if one. Instantly his men and the crew of the enemy careened over their ships' rails and began hand-to-hand combat, the patriots using musket butts, axes, hatchets, pitchforks—whatever weapons were at their disposal. Fortunately, from what Treadwell could see, his crew did not appear to be outnumbered.

Hut leapt aboard the enemy vessel, his massive frame plowing its way through several sailors. He handily swung his musket butt like a club, delivering blows that toppled men, none of whom rose again.

Caleb followed Hut over the rails, cutlass in hand, as he peered through the smoke in search of an enemy combatant. He did not have to search long as he was immediately pounced upon and knocked down by a Brit, his musket brought down hard across Caleb's windpipe. Struggling for air, Caleb used his legs to lift his torso to throw off his attacker, but the man was too heavy. With what should have been his last breath, Caleb wielded his cutlass and stabbed his enemy in the side, thrusting his knife over and over as his attacker lost strength with each blow. Finally Caleb shoved the gasping and wounded soldier to the side, righted himself and moved across the deck.

Jacob stayed on board the *Josephine,* keeping close to Treadwell to help ward off any attacks on his captain, his prosthetic hook always at the ready to be sunk into the arm, leg or throat of any assailant. But before Jacob had a chance to defend the captain, a musket ball whizzed past him and into the thigh of the captain, who stumbled back onto the deck, grasping his thigh, as blood pooled beneath him. Jacob immediately removed his tunic and tied it around Treadwell's leg to stop the bleeding. He propped the captain up against the main mast, then turned to survey the situation. In spite of the injury sustained by Treadwell, it was evident the fight was turning in their favor. Treadwell could see it, too.

"Shout out to them to strike their colors," he told Jacob, as he did not have the strength to do it himself.

"Strike your colors!" Jacob yelled across to the embattled enemy. "Strike your colors if you care to see the end of this day!" The Brits waited for their commander to make his call. Seeing that his men were outnumbered, with several wounded and possibly dying, the captain of the British vessel gave the order to cease fighting and to strike their colors in surrender. The British dropped their weapons. The crew of the *Josephine* gathered them up and began leading the men to the hold.

In his exuberance, Caleb jumped atop the bulwarks, cheering the surrender with his fellow Sons of Liberty. His broad smile beamed and his face glistened with sweat, a slight breeze causing his tunic sleeves to billow. A sudden shift in the wind jostled the ships and sent him grasping for the rope ladder nearby, but just out of reach. He waved his arms frantically to catch his balance as Hut raced across the deck to grab him, but it was too late. Caleb's scream of despair was silenced as soon as his body hit the sluicing, ink-black water of Long Island Sound. Hut, Jacob and several other men leaned over the railings, peering into the waters below as the ships continued to move on their way, but there was no sign of Caleb. Hut and Jacob stared at each other. Had they sighted him, they could have thrown him a rope.

"Do you know if he can swim?" Hut asked, hopeful that Caleb could possibly survive, and knowing if it were him, he would definitely succumb to the waters.

"I don't know, Hut," came Jacob's despairing answer as the two men stared at the water in disbelief at what had just occurred. Jacob immediately wondered how he would tell Mehti, or Caleb's family.

The fight had lasted no more than a half hourglass. The British toll was several wounded and one dead. The patriots fared better, with a few wounded and no casualties, with the probable exception of Caleb Rogers.

Chapter 18

Rebecca called to Mehti from across the yard, excitedly waving the second letter from Frederic above her head. She sat on the bench that circled the large apple tree between the house and barn, and waited for Mehti to join her. Now that she realized she and her sister were of the same circumstances, she wanted to share every bit of news with Mehti in the hope they could be closer and supportive of one another in the absence of the men they cared about.

Oliver stood at Rebecca's feet, his arms held over his head, a request to be lifted onto the bench. He liked to travel from one side of the bench to the other, peeking around the tree trunk on each side, laughing every time she would call out, "Boo." It was a game he could play for hours, and it occurred to Rebecca she was so grateful for such a happy, contented, albeit active, child.

Mehti joined her sister on the bench. "What did you receive?"

"It's my second letter from Frederic, just two weeks after the first," she said with a burst of excitement, her eyes vibrant with joy as if lit from within.

"Oh, please read it to me," Mehti said, trying to hide the concern she felt because Hut, Jacob and Caleb had still not returned.

Rebecca read her sister's expression and laid her hand upon Mehti's. "All will be well, Mehti. Trust me, Hut and Jacob would not let anything happen to Caleb. And neither would Captain Treadwell."

Mehti felt her sister's reassurance and settled comfortably onto the bench to listen to her read.

Rebecca noticed Oliver was enthralled with a beetle that had found its way onto the bench, so she knew she had some time to focus on her letter.

August 10, 1781

My dearest Rebecca,

I write again because I anticipate the days are mounting when we will begin our march south through New Jersey and on to Baltimore, then Philadelphia. Our eventual destination is a place called Yorktown. I am told we will leave behind some Continentals encamped to convince the British our intent is to attack New York.

My hope is we will be received along the way as well as we had been traversing Connecticut where people stood along the roadside, handing us bread, cheeses, jellies and jams. They also provided us with cider, buttermilk and a delicious rum made from cherries. In one town where we camped, a band played, and a ball was organized to entertain the troops. I suspect such comforts will not prevail as we continue our march. But one never knows. These experiences in America are quite new to us all. The support we have received buoys our spirits.

I am uncertain when I will be able to write again. Please know that I think of you every day and your image alone keeps my spirits alive. My best to your family.

With much affection,
Frederic

Rebecca lifted the letter to her nose and inhaled, a smile easing across her face. The scent of gun oil was all she could discern, but it was enough to cause him to feel near.

"Yorktown!" Mehti exclaimed. "I shudder to think of battle brewing in the heat of Virginia this time of year."

"I imagine the marching must be quite exhausting. I've heard some men say they prefer battle to marching."

And on that word, as had happened so many times since the war started, they looked to the south to see the silhouettes of two horses sauntering up over the rise, carrying two riders. Rebecca saw them first, as Mehti was focusing her attention on Oliver. One rider sat tall and broad in the saddle; the other was smaller and slightly hunched. Then Mehti saw them. The sisters locked eyes, the unspoken question lingering in the air between them like a puff of smoke, but neither dared speak it. *Who is not returning?*

Finally Mehti said something. "I think that's Hut on Maisey." She swallowed hard.

"Yes, I think you're right." The two stared intently, as if doing so would bring the other rider's image more quickly into focus.

"It's Jacob," Mehti said, her heart in a whirl of emotions. Her brother was safe. But what of Caleb?

The women's eyes locked again and Rebecca could see the angst in Mehti's eyes.

"Perhaps Caleb stayed behind," she said encouragingly.

Rebecca lifted Oliver and the two women hurried toward the riders, meeting them halfway. Jacob stared down at his mount, Caleb's horse. Hut looked off into the distance, not able to make eye contact with either of the women.

Mehti mustered her courage to speak. "What of Caleb?"

Hut did not answer her immediately, but stepped down from Maisey and gathered the reins. He had wondered all the way from New London what he would say to Mehti. And Jacob mulled over how he would tell Caleb's parents of the loss.

"We took a British vessel near Long Island," Hut began, measuring his words. "Master Caleb, he fought a good fight. He be very brave. But he fell into dat water and he never come up. We could not see him to even try to save him. He was gone so fast and de boat was moving."

"Did the ship circle back?" Mehti asked, her voice pitched and cracking.

"No, Mehti. We could not turn de boats. They were bound together. I am sorry, Mehti, but Caleb, he gone."

Mehti's mind began its search of any scenario that would mean Caleb was still alive. "Where did the battle take place? How far from shore was the boat?" she asked both men, her eyes darting from one to the other. "Caleb is an excellent swimmer, Hut. He's nothing like you. He could have swum to shore," she exclaimed.

"The fight was near the north shore," Jacob said. "But we were half a mile from there and I don't think even a strong swimmer could make that distance, especially after being in battle," he reasoned.

"Why are you giving up?' Mehti shouted at Jacob in exasperation. "He could have made it to shore. We have to go look for him!"

"At the north fork of Long Island?" Jacob shook his head. "That area is swarming with Redcoats. I understand you're distressed, Mehti, but you have to face the fact that Caleb is gone," he said gently. "I'm sorry."

Mehti spun around, determination and fury taking command of her. "I will find him. I need to get a boat suitable to cross the Sound." Her cheeks were burning in angst as she strode toward the house. She turned to them all and shouted, "People don't just disappear! I will find him, either way."

"Mehti," Hut called after her. "Where would you even begin to look? Long Island Sound is very big. And dat coast is very long. I understand you are upset, but you need to tink dis trou'."

"Won't you help me, Hut?"

"Oh yes, dat would look good, a young girl and a black man traveling together, asking questions 'bout a missing privateer dat maybe drown at sea."

"I will ask my father," she said stubbornly.

"And he will tell you da same ting. Tink 'bout dis, Miss Mehti. If Caleb made it to da shore, he would be seen. Maybe he be helped. If dere is any way he could get back home, he would come. Da worse ting to happen would be if dem Loyalists get dey hands on him. And if dey did, what could you or I, or even your daddy, do? No, Mehti, you have to stay here and wait. If he can, he will come. If he drown, he will never come."

"But then I will never know. I will sit here, day after day, not knowing if he is dead or alive. That will be torture, Hut." Mehti began to cry and Hut took the liberty to pull her to him to comfort her.

"We can ask your father, but I 'spec he will agree wit me and Jacob. But you can pray for him to come home Mehti."

"If I thought it would do any good, I would spend every minute of every day praying for his return," Mehti said with skepticism.

Chapter 19

Since the loss of Caleb Rogers, the somber mood in both the White and Rogers households, hung heavily over them all like a thick, suffocating fog that made it hard to breathe. Mehti found she could not focus on her chores. Even the children's play did not lift her spirits as it normally would. Malcolm, now six months old and crawling, would charge across the kitchen floor, head down, to chase a cackling, swift-moving Oliver and timid Abigail, all of them oblivious to the emotional pain the adults were feeling. Try as Malcolm might to catch them, he never could. But the expended effort guaranteed an afternoon nap and an opportunity for Ruby to churn, sew or milk. The children's play usually made Mehti laugh, but not now.

Whenever Maisey was available, Mehti would ride to the beach at General Neck in New London, her spyglass in hand, to search the waters, not only for the British, but for Caleb as well. She combed the beach on the off chance he would appear, uncertain if she wanted him found. Finding him on the beach would mean she had found his body, a vision she would immediately put out of her mind. Rather, she fantasized seeing him walk up out of the water, a desired miracle, which of course was not possible. From time to time she would make her way into the city and visit with Ruth and old man Cuthbert, quizzing them about any strangers entering their store with tales of a young blond lad taken captive or washed ashore. Each time they let her know with deep sympathy that they had heard nothing.

She dared to walk out on the docks, unescorted, to question sailors, known and unknown to her, whether they had seen or heard anything of Caleb. Their repetitive, negative headshakes recurred in her nightmares, taunting her over and over again. On such nights, she would wake in a sweat, filled with anxiety, her heart palpitating in her chest like the heart of a wounded and frightened sparrow.

One restless night, unable to sleep in the stifling heat, brazenly barefooted she threw on her robe in her bed chamber, descended the stairs and stepped outside into the cool night air. She sat on the stoop and breathed deeply, trying to calm herself. Staring up at the moon, she wondered if Caleb were alive somewhere and looking up at the moon as well. Then out of the corner of her eye, she saw some movement and shifted her gaze to the right, along a hedgerow, straining to see. *Animal or human?* It could be a deer, or a bear, and wolves were still sighted from time to time. But this creature appeared to be taller, perhaps hunched over.

Mehti was torn between fear for her safety and her curiosity. It was clear the trespasser, whoever or whatever it was, did not realize she was sitting, still as a statue on the stoop, not more than three rods away. Finally, she made out the silhouette of a man who appeared to be holding something in his hand. A shift in the wind carried the aroma of whale oil across the yard as the man crouched down and placed the object on the ground. She was mesmerized, unable to move or yell out, uncertain of the man's intentions.

She heard the striking of flint and, within seconds the object on the ground, a torch, was aflame, emitting a crackling noise and a glow that lit up the contorted face of Mordecai Greeley. Mehti gasped, immediately concerned that she had given herself away. But Mordecai seemed to take no notice of her. Any other time, she would have called to him, asking what his purpose was to be on their property in the middle of the night. His hair was in disarray and he seemed to be mumbling to himself. The fiendish look on his face in the glow of firelight gave her pause, froze her voice and kept her silent. Mehti's mind raced about what to do next. She needed to get help. Her father, Jacob, Rachael and Abigail, along with Rebecca and Oliver, were asleep in the house. Hut, Ruby, baby Malcolm, Jon Bear and her Aunt Sarah were asleep in their living quarters in the barn annex.

Mordecai grabbed the torch and, hunched over, began to move swiftly down the side of their property, following the hedgerow toward the back of the house. As soon as he was out of sight, Mehti jumped up, opened the front door and ran up the stairs as fast as she could. Where once she was frightened with anxiety, she now was riddled with fear of impending disaster. She felt sure her family was in danger, but had no idea why Mordecai was skulking through their property.

She pounded first on her father's bedchamber door. "Father, Father," she called out to him with urgency. His hearing had degraded so much in the last few years, she was concerned he could not hear her pleas. When he did not respond, she moved on to Jacob and Rachael's bed chamber door.

"Jacob! Rachael!" she yelled. Then she heard Abigail begin to cry, "Mommy, Mommy!"

Jacob immediately swung open the door as he pulled his robe on over his night shirt. Mehti could see Rachael in the room, on the edge of their bed, comforting Abigail to not be afraid.

"Mehti, what on earth is going on? Have you lost your wits?" Jacob scolded. "What sort of Tomfoolery is this?"

"Jacob, I think something is amiss! I have just been out on the stoop and witnessed Mordecai Greeley with a lit torch in his hand. He is prowling around and gone to the back of the house. I think he is not in his right mind, Jacob! Father is not answering. We must do something!"

Rebecca, who had been roused from her sleep by the clamor in the hallway, stepped out of her room, quietly closing the door behind her, lest Oliver be awakened.

"What's happening?" she asked Mehti and Jacob.

"It's Mordecai," Mehti exclaimed. "He's on our property in the middle of the night and acting very peculiar. It's frightening to see him, Rebecca. He's behaving so strangely."

"Yes, I have seen him of late and I agree he seems quite unhinged."

"You both stay here," Jacob instructed. "I will go and find Mordecai."

Jacob donned his house shoes and made his way out the front door. The moon gave enough light that, once his eyes adjusted to the darkness, it was easy for him to make his way around the side of the house, past the kitchen garden. The smell of smoke permeating the air told Jacob that Mordecai could not be far off. Turning the back corner, where the field sloped away from their house, he caught sight of Mordecai blithely setting the torch flame to the grasses along the edge the house. With each touch of the torch, a burst of flames billowed skyward, casting an eerie glow on Mordecai's face. He appeared to be chanting or mumbling to himself as he went about his task.

Jacob felt a rush of alarm. "Mordecai!" he cried out. "What evil is this?" he yelled as he rushed toward him.

As Jacob closed in on him, Mordecai turned serenely toward Jacob, as if in a trance. While his demeanor was calm, the frenzy in his eyes quickly revealed his madness. "I am not the evil one here, but evil lurks within," he yelled at Jacob as he raised his torch and pointed toward the house. He turned dismissively and continued lighting the fires, as if on a mission of destiny no mere mortal could interrupt.

Jacob reached Mordecai, shoved him to the ground and immediately began stomping out the torch flame beside him.

"You fool!" Mordecai yelled up at Jacob. "I do God's work!" He leapt to his feet and the two men tussled, Jacob unable to hold on to the older man, who seemingly possessed the strength of two or three men. Finally, Jacob shoved Mordecai away from him and turned to tend to the fire that had begun to consume the house along its lowest clapboards.

Mordecai stumbled backward against the burning house, the back of his tunic catching fire. Realizing his clothes had caught, he began to cry out in panic and fear. The whale oil he'd inadvertently splashed on his clothes lit, quickly consuming him. Jacob tried to approach Mordecai, who suddenly stopped screaming and stood perfectly still, as if accepting his fate.

He raised his arms to the sky and called out, "I will end this torment!" Jacob removed his robe and, holding it in front of him to ward off the heat of the flames, repeatedly tried to get close enough to snuff out the flames. Finally, he knocked Mordecai to the ground and managed to smother the engulfing flames with his robe.

From around the other side of the house, Jacob could see Hut and Jon Bear rushing toward him with buckets of water. Mehti had gone to them for help as soon as the smell of rising smoke reached their second-story windows. Jacob left Mordecai and grabbed a bucket; along with Jon Bear, he began dowsing the flames on the back of the house while Hut ran back to the well for more water. Within half an hour, the fire was out and Hut, Jacob and Jon Bear collapsed to the ground, relieved and exhausted.

The men looked over at the crumpled, motionless body of Mordecai Greely, smoke still rising from the robe that covered him. While Jacob knew for certain he was gone, Hut walked over and tried to lift the robe; but he could not separate it, since it had adhered to Greely's burned and blistered body.

Rebecca and Rachael, holding fast to Oliver and Abigail, had kept their distance throughout the ordeal, while Mehti helped haul water. When it was over, they moved closer, mystified by what had happened. Mehti explained what she knew of Mordecai's trespassing, and Rebecca told everyone of the odd behavior he displayed just a week earlier.

"I believe he thought you possessed, Rebecca," Jacob said.

"We must say nothing of this," Jon Bear said sternly, looking around at the circle of family gathered. "I will explain to your father in the morning about Mordecai's purpose to do harm and explain that he seemed to have lost his mind, holding hard feelings at his rejection. But nothing of his outlandish claims against Rebecca. It is best we do not speak of it."

Everyone nodded in agreement.

Shaken at the prospect of Mordecai's accusations, Rebecca recalled the recent incident of Mordecai standing in front of the house, scowling and displaying a cross in her direction. She kissed Oliver's forehead as he drifted back to sleep in her arms, grateful her son was safe from so horrid a man. Then the women left the gathering and slowly returned to the house, all of them in a state of shock by the night's events.

Chapter 20

Baiting Hollow occupied a stretch of coast on the north fork of Long Island, edged with miles of beach surrounded by marshlands and fields. Several farmers helped each other bring in hay from the marsh or harvest the fields, at least up until the Battle of Brooklyn Heights in the summer of '76. Then the purpose of eastern Long Island became simply to supply the needs of the British Army.

When the British occupied much of Long Island after that battle, many male patriots fled to Connecticut. They left their wives and children behind in hopes the Brits would leave them to live off that land, however impoverished they might end up. And so it was with the Cummings family.

Every other morning, five-year old Maggie and seven-year old William Cummings left their home in the early morning to comb the beaches of Baiting Hollow to collect driftwood that had come ashore the previous night. Once dried out, it proved to be a reliable fuel source for cooking. The few trees that remained in the area had been felled and transported to New York for the benefit of the British Army. Driftwood, dried seaweed and dried cow chips were their only remaining sources of fuel.

"Wait up!" little Maggie called after her brother. William pulled the two-handled cart behind him, stopping on occasion to toss in a piece of wood while Maggie gathered what would be used for kindling—smaller pieces of wood and hunks of seaweed. The cart was just the right size for William to handle, its two big wheels sometimes getting stuck in the sand if he underestimated the weight of their haul. Generally he managed by himself, but if the cart got too heavy, Maggie would take one side and William the other.

The two scavengers headed east, Long Island Sound to their left, marsh grass to their right and the rising sun in their faces. Maggie's bonnet protected her head from the increasing heat and the glare of light that angled toward them. As they walked along, William would hum a hymn from church services. His favorite was "Be Still My Soul," and Maggie would try to remember the words, but usually could only sing the first line—*"Be still thy soul, the Lord is on thy side."* Then she would hum along with William until the next verse and repeat the familiar words over.

William was humming the tune when all of a sudden he stopped abruptly, mid-stanza. He raised his hand to shield his eyes and peered off up the beach. Something was there but he couldn't make out what it was—perhaps a large piece of driftwood, or maybe two.

Maggie strained to see as well. "What is it, William?"

"I...I'm not sure," he stammered.

The object, or objects, lay about four rods ahead of them on the beach.

"Let's go see what it is, William," Maggie said and began racing ahead of him down the beach.

"Maggie, wait!" William yelled after her as he lay down the cart handles and ran after her. When the two of them got within a rod of the objects, William could see that what lay on the beach was the body of a man lying on his stomach, his head facing away from them. William instinctively stood between Maggie and the body in an attempt to protect his sister from what could be a grisly sight. It was clear to him that a body had washed up on shore, its clothing appearing wet. From this distance all he could make out was a cluster of matted blond hair, and a large piece of driftwood alongside the body. He noted the man's feet were bare and his clothing askew.

Looking around, William picked up a nearby stick and grasped it tightly, as if it were a sword, ready to protect them should the intruder leap up in an attack. He could feel his heart pounding. The two cautiously stepped closer and closer to the still body, Maggie tiptoeing behind her brother and peering around him from side to side.

When they were close enough, William leaned forward and, holding his breath, poked at the body with his stick. There was no response. He poked again; still no response. He breathed a sigh of relief.

"It's all right, Maggie, he's dead. Help me turn him over— see if we know who it is."

The two of them walked around the body, knelt down and pushed as hard as they could to flip the man's body so he would be lying on his back. It took them three tries and finally the body rolled slightly and landed face up. Now William could see it was not a man, but perhaps a teenage boy.

"We need to go tell Mom," Maggie said, looking up at her brother. All of a sudden, the body groaned and the boy's sand-caked eyelids began to flutter.

"Eeeeek!" Maggie screamed simultaneously with William, who dropped his stick and jumped back. The two began running down the beach as fast as they could, leaving the cart and driftwood behind. They ran without looking back until they reached the cart path that led along the edge of the marsh grass then along the planted fields. Only then did William look back to make sure Maggie wasn't too far behind. He stopped to catch his breath and give her time to catch up. William could see his mother not far off, a pitchfork in her hands, harvesting potatoes in the field. Maggie and William ran up to her, both gasping for air from their run. William grabbed his mother's hand and started pulling her toward the cart path.

"Mother, come quickly! There's a boy... er a man... washed up on shore. He's down at the beach and he's alive! You have to come quick. I don't know who he is."

His mother pulled back her arm. "William, wait just a moment and catch your breath. Now, slowly, tell me what this is all about," she said, seeming unconvinced there was a real emergency.

William took a deep breath. "Mother, we were halfway down the beach, collecting driftwood and we saw something and went to see it close up. When we got to it, it was the body of a young man, or a boy, I'm not sure which. I was sure he was dead— maybe drowned or something. But when we turned him over onto his back, his eyes opened and he groaned. So he's not dead." He paused and took another deep breath. "But it scared us so much we came running home. But we can go back and help him, Mother. So you have to come," he pleaded as he grabbed her arm again. Maggie grabbed her other arm.

The three made their way across the field and down the cart path, back onto the beach walking at a quick pace. "Hurry, Mother," William urged as he was several steps in front of her.

But his pace slowed before they reached spot where they had left the cart, because beyond it lay only the piece of driftwood. The young man who had made it to shore was gone, leaving behind only an indentation in the sand and footprints that led off into the marsh.

William's mother looked toward the marsh as her son grabbed her by the hand. "Mother, we need to go find him. He may need our help."

She hesitated, not wanting to put herself or her children at risk. She knelt down to speak to William. "I'm sure he will be well, William. Obviously, if he was able to get up and walk away, he's well enough to make his way to get the help he needs. Come now, bring your cart. I must get back to the potatoes before the day becomes too hot to harvest."

Chapter 21

Caleb crouched among the tall marsh grasses, peering between them at a woman and two children who were gazing down at the spot on the beach he had occupied just minutes before. He realized his footprints led directly into the marsh, but there was nothing he could do about that now. It was possible if the woman found him, she would be able to help him with food and water—maybe even a way home. He debated whether to make his whereabouts known to her and decided against it. She could be a Loyalist, in which case he would be at risk of having his presence divulged to the British.

He craned to hear their conversation, but could not make out their words over the sound of the waves, especially from this distance. He breathed a sigh of relief when at last they turned and headed back down the beach, whence they had come. Caleb sat back to rest a moment. He saw the sun was rising to his right as he faced the water. It meant he was not in Connecticut, but on Long Island. He waited some time to be sure it was on the rise, and it was. But where he was on the island, he had no idea. He was thirsty and decided his first task would be to find a fresh stream.

His memory was cloudy and he strained to recollect his thoughts. He recalled the victory at sea, falling overboard and being drawn down into the depths of the Sound in the ship's wake, the undertow sucking the shoes off his feet. He struggled to the surface, gasping for air, only to search the dark horizon to see— nothing. He could hear men's voices in the distance as the sound traveled over the water, but visually, all was black.

The waters of the Sound were cool, but not cold, and he was thankful for that. The chop was lolling, another saving grace. He recalled treading water for what seemed like hours. At the time of the encounter with the British vessel, the ships were closer to Long Island than to Connecticut, so he determined to try to swim toward the island. He located the North Star and headed in the opposite direction, sometimes floating on his back. His arms and legs became so heavy, so tired, he eventually was only able to float, kicking sporadically just to keep himself above water.

Lying on his back, he'd gazed up at the night sky and a glorious moon. He wondered whether Mehti was looking up at the moon as well, but realized it was unlikely in the middle of the night. But the thought warmed him and strengthened his resolve to make it to shore. The waves began to lap over his face, a sign he was losing buoyancy. Then an amazing thing happened. A large piece of driftwood rolled toward him, unsolicited. He grabbed onto it and managed to hoist his body lengthwise onto the log. He lay on his stomach, his arms and legs dangling in the water, and lay his head down to rest. The next thing he knew, he was being rolled over; he opened his eyes to see and hear two children scream in panic and run off. He had apparently washed up on shore during the night.

He had hoisted himself up and stiffly headed toward the tall marsh cattails on the edge of the beach. His legs felt like they were weighted down with ballast.

After locating a fresh brook that fed into the marshland, Caleb not only drank his fill, but bathed in the shallow waters to rinse the salt from his hair, body and clothes. He determined his best course would be to find the nearest path or cart way and travel south, if at all possible. He recalled his shipmates' talk about ports on the south side of Long Island. Skirting some farmland, he came upon a cart path that headed east/west and decided to head east. By high noon, his clothes were quite dry. After walking for what he guessed was a few hours, he came upon a fork in the road—the right fork heading south, the left heading straight on— and decided to head south. While he passed by numerous planted fields in his travels, fortunately he never encountered another person.

Coming up over a rise at a relative clearing, he caught his first glimpse of water that he believed bordered the south side of Long Island and felt the ocean breezes that swept upland. To his left, golden salt hay, waiting for a fall scythe, were laid back by the constant winds.

Caleb found it puzzling that the body of water before him seemed to be a huge bay that contained another body of land, perhaps an island. In the cradle of the bay just below him, he could discern several buildings and a long wharf with two ships tied alongside. From this distance, he could see a young boy sitting on the edge of the dock, fishing. A few crewmen were making their way up and down the wharf. He picked up his pace, heading for the hamlet, all the while rehearsing what he might say if questioned about who he was and where he came from.

Entering the village, he noticed an old man sitting on a barrel in front of a building, whittling on a piece of wood. His sparse, tobacco-stained, white beard fell to the middle of his sunken chest. His slight frame was all but lost in the folds of his worn homespun tunic, which Caleb believed he must have filled out at one time. Homespun was a good sign the man was a Patriot.

"Good morning, sir," Caleb began as he looked down at the old man.

"Morning. And who might you be?" the man slurred through a toothless mouth.

"Caleb. Caleb Rogers. I wonder if you could tell me the name of this place."

"You don't know where you are?"

"No sir, unfortunately, I do not."

"What did you do, fall off a ship?" the man said, throwing his head back in laughter, exposing his pink gums and thinking he had made a joke.

"Well, that is exactly what happened to me, in the middle of the night. My captain wasn't able to get to me," Caleb responded. He looked around at the buildings in the village, trying to get his bearings. He noticed the man was sitting in front of a tavern/store with a painted sign overhead that read, "Stirling Village Tavern and Goods."

"You are in Stirling," the old man said, pointing up at the sign behind him.

"And what is this body of water, and that land?" Caleb asked pointing at the bay.

"That be Shelter Harbor Island and that be Gardiner Bay. And who is your captain?"

"Captain Treadwell out of New London."

"Oh yes, the *Josephine*. I know it well. Been docked here more than once over the years," the old man responded. Then he whispered, "He's a Patriot."

"Yes sir," Caleb responded proudly and with a sigh of relief, certain he and the old man were on the same side. Now the old man started volunteering information.

"Down on the dock you can see the *Rose*. It's a private cargo ship—been here for four days, loading up on supplies and is about to disembark. In front of that is the *HMS Barbuda*. It's been here two months, under repair. So if you are looking for a way to get back to Connecticut, I recommend you see the captain of the *Rose*."

"I thank you, sir," Caleb said as he headed for the wharf. He thought a moment about asking the old man where he might get something to eat, then thought better of it. If he could get hired on to the *Rose*, a meal could be in the offing.

"God speed," the old man said, returning to his whittling.

With trepidation, Caleb walked past the *Barbuda*, trying his best to be inconspicuous. He made his way up the gangway and stepped down onto the deck. The *Rose* was a sloop like the *Josephine*, so Caleb felt right at home.

"Are you looking for someone?" a voice called out from behind him. Caleb turned to see a middle-aged man about his height with salt-and-pepper hair and matching beard, and a width that could compete with his height.

"I'm looking for the captain," Caleb said.

"You're looking at the captain, son. Captain James."

Caleb proceeded to share his dilemma with the captain and asked if his ship would be sailing to Connecticut. He hoped to work for passage.

Captain James looked Caleb over and scratched his wooly beard. "We'll be going to Connecticut," he replied.

"Could I work for my passage? I've had some experience working on a vessel just like this one, the *Josephine*. Do you know of it?"

"I can't say that I know of that ship. But you look like a strapping young man, and we could use a hand. I'll bet you're hungry," he said. Then glancing down at Caleb's feet, he added, "I suspect you could use a pair of shoes, as well."

Caleb was delighted by the captain's generosity and willingness to take him in. "Yes, sir. Thank you, sir."

"We'll be leaving in a few hours," the captain said, looking skyward. "The winds are right. Go down below and tell Cook you're coming on board and he'll fix you something to eat."

"Thank you, sir," Caleb said, beaming over his good fortune.

Caleb went below and was given a tin of beans with bread, which he ate topside, sitting on the deck at the ship's stern. He was feeling a bit guilty about sitting and eating while he watched the crew prepare the ship for departure. Finally, he finished and began helping the crew in hoisting the sails. A slight breeze took hold of the sails and they were underway, immediately sailing past Shelter Harbor Island and out facing the Atlantic. Caleb watched as the ship slowly turned to starboard and headed south. He leaned over to one of the crewmen and asked why the captain maneuvered the ship in that direction. Perhaps there were shoals to bypass.

"That's the direction we're heading in—Jamaica," the sailor replied with a smile.

"Jamaica? I thought this ship was heading to Connecticut?" Caleb said, a feeling of panic overtaking him.

"Oh, we'll get to Connecticut... on the return voyage."

Caleb could feel his stomach turning as he ran to the ship's rail and lost his meal to the ocean. He wiped his mouth with his sleeve and looked up in disbelief at the ever-shrinking coast of Long Island.

Chapter 22

Late August brought stifling heat to Granville and, indeed, to most of Connecticut, Rhode Island and Massachusetts. As Rebecca and Mehti headed out to the fields to help harvest the corn, Rebecca tried to imagine what it must be like for Washington and his army to be marching through the southern latitudes where she imagined temperatures must be ever so brutal. While she hadn't received another letter from Frederic since his description of the army's march through Philadelphia, she overheard the men in the tavern talking about troop movement.

"What of the French cavalry?" she asked.

"The armies are moving together and heading south," was the only information they would offer, something she already knew.

Jacob, Hut and Gabriel had been to the fields since before sun up and their silhouettes were visible among the corn stalks just at the rise as they wielded their sickles. Nearby stood Maisey and the mule harnessed to the wagon. They automatically moved along with the workers as stalks of corn were loaded. Rebecca and Mehti bypassed Jon Bear napping on the bench under the apple tree. He had been able to work through the night due to a harvest moon that made night seem almost like day.

"I should like to go to New London tomorrow," Mehti said hesitantly, glancing over to gauge Rebecca's reaction. "That is, of course, if we get our work done today. I'm sure Ruthie would welcome a visit from you," she added to sweeten her suggestion. Of late, Rebecca seemed reluctant to encourage Mehti's trips to New London, concerned that Mehti should start to move on with her life and accept the likelihood that Caleb had perished—a part of the sea now. Rebecca did not respond.

"It gives me peace of mind to go to General Neck and keep a lookout. And you know that visiting the docks always gives me hope. I feel it is something I must do." Again, Rebecca was silent.

"You are so fortunate, Rebecca, really, to know that Frederic is alive and with his fellow cavalrymen. It must be a comfort to you to feel he exists someplace on this earth while I sit and wonder. I cannot accept that Caleb is gone and I feel compelled to not give up my search for him," she said pleadingly.

"Mehti, I spoke just yesterday with Caleb's mother. They have accepted that their son is gone. They do not go to the beach, searching. They do not go to the wharves to ask after him. You are causing yourself so much torment. You would be much better off to just accept what has likely become his fate."

The two young women stopped and looked into each other's eyes as they had done so frequently of late. It seemed to Rebecca that Mehti had aged tremendously in just the last month.

135

Her once-joyous expression now carried a perpetual frown of concern. Now her light-brown eyes always seemed sad, lacking their usual glint of mischief.

"I worry only for you," Rebecca said as she brushed a wisp of hair the color of maple sugar from her sister's face.

"So can we go?" Mehti asked, undaunted.

Just then a frantic call came from Jacob, and where there had been three silhouettes, there now stood two. Rebecca and Mehti rushed through the cornstalk stubble toward them. Jacob and Hut were bent over Gabriel, who lay crumpled on the ground, grabbing at his ankle, Hut tore away the fabric from Gabriel's trousers as blood began to pool under Gabriel's legs.

"Your apron!" Jacob commanded, pointing to Mehti's clothes.

Mehti quickly removed her apron as Rebecca sat down and, lifting her father's head, cradled it in her lap. His frightened eyes gazed up at hers.

"You will be fine, Father. It will be fine," Rebecca said in a soothing voice, trying to quell his fears.

Hut grabbed the apron from Mehti. Moving Gabriel's hand from around his ankle, he grimaced as he saw spurts of blood pulsing from a deep gash where Gabriel's sickle had sliced into his flesh. Hut quickly wrapped the apron around the wound to stop the blood flow, but in seconds the fabric absorbed the blood and continued pooling. Jacob quickly removed a trouser tie and handed it to Hut.

"Wrap this over the fabric and pull it tight," he told Hut. "The pressure should help stop the flow. Just make it as tight as you can." Although he tried to remain calm, he noticed the rise in his voice. The fabric continued to absorb blood and the pooling was ever increasing.

"Becca?" Gabriel said faintly as his questioning eyes looked into hers one last time.

She watched the color drain from his face before his eyes closed and his body slackened.

"Father?" Becca said, patting his cheek. "Father, you must open your eyes. You must stay awake," she said, staring down at his serene face.

Mehti stood watching the entire event in disbelief. Only a few moments had passed before their father became what she thought was unconscious.

Hut and Jacob looked at each other and sat back among the corn stubble.

"What are you doing? You have to do something!" Mehti yelled at Hut. His deep chocolate skin was glistening with sweat.

"Miss Mehti, do you see all dat blood?" Hut asked, pointing to the large mass of blood under Gabriel's body. "Do you see dat a man cannot lose all dat blood and still live?"

Rebecca bent down and kissed her father's still-warm forehead as tears streamed down her cheeks and landed in her father's thinning hair.

Mehti began crying, as well; but amid her sadness, anger took hold. "How much more death can we manage? First it was Mr. Greeley, then it was... it was... it was Caleb," she stammered, struggling to acknowledge his death. "And now Father! I don't know how much more of this I can stand!" She turned abruptly and ran through the field toward the house.

"Mehti!" Rebecca called after her. She wanted to go to her sister, but found she was unable to leave her father. The three sat for a long time before Hut stood up and walked to the wagon to begin unloading the harvested corn stalks. The wagon would now be serving another purpose.

Chapter 23

For days afterward, the White household, along with the entire Granville community, remained wrapped in solemnness, recovering from shock at Gabriel White's sudden death. His burial took place the day after he died, and now three rudimentary markers stood on the hillock beyond the barn—Gabriel's, his wife Anna's, and baby Anna's, the infant daughter of Jacob and Rachael.

That first evening meal after Gabriel's burial, the family members stood at their usual places, including Jacob, until he realized no one was sitting. "Shall we not sit and partake of our meal?" he asked, looking around at his motionless family.

"It is your turn at the head," Rebecca replied.

Jacob hesitated. With the flurry of events since Father's death, it had not occurred to him he would now be the head of the family. His father had held prominence in this household. He had been a force to be reckoned with at times, but was always respected by family and friends. His strength of character served as a foundation of security for them all. Jacob could not imagine himself filling the void left by his father. He glanced around the table and received a nod of approval from Mehti. Hut and Ruby were taking dinner in their barn annex, but Aunt Sarah and Jon Bear were standing at the table, their expressions likewise signaling approval.

"It is time, Jacob," Aunt Sarah assured him.

Jacob nodded and stepped to the head of the table, taking what had been his father's seat. Then the rest of the family took their seats, and everyone settled into the safe feelings accorded by continuity. They clasped hands and Jacob began the blessing as his father had always done at the main meal. He ended the blessing by adding, "And God please bless our unborn and allow it to enter this world a healthy baby." Jacob glanced around the table at the wide-eyed expressions on the faces of his family."

"Rachael is with child?" Rebecca said with excitement.

"Yes—we just got word yesterday. I didn't want to say anything with Father's passing, but the timing seemed appropriate now," Jacob said, passing the beans.

"A new playmate for Abigail, Oliver and Malcom! How exciting!" Mehti said.

"Let's not get ahead of ourselves," Jacob cautioned. "The doctor estimates Rachael is due in mid-winter, and that's a long way from now." Jacob looked to his wife and noticed she was blushing. Rebecca and Mehti jumped up immediately to give their sister-in-law an embrace.

"Do you notice that when one soul leaves us, another takes its place? I think it is God's work to help alleviate the pain of our loss," Aunt Sarah exclaimed.

The good news of the impending addition to the family lifted everyone's spirits as they enjoyed their meal.

Two days later, Mehti, Rebecca and Hut left Granville by wagon before sunrise, in order to arrive New London in the early-morning hours. The trip was quiet, all three riders seemingly deep in thought along the way. Even the mule and Maisey seemed more subdued.

When they arrived at the butcher shop, Hut expressed concern that old man Cuthbert would be perturbed at his absence over the last few days, but word had spread about Gabriel's sudden death.

"Sorry to hear about Gabriel," old man Cuthbert said as he stared down at the floor. Hut just nodded and went right to his butchering. Rebecca went into the grocery store to help Ruthie Cuthbert shelve items that had been delivered the day before, while Mehti unharnessed the mule and Maisey.

"I would like to head to the beach at General Neck," Mehti announced after sharing greetings with Ruthie.

"Are you not planning on visiting the docks?" Rebecca asked.

Mehti thought it over. "Not today. I feel a need to head to the General Neck for some reason."

"Well, we could go down and ask after Caleb," Ruthie told her. She felt such compassion for the girl since Caleb's disappearance. Reaching to find Rebecca, she took hold of her arm and added, "I get out so seldom, it would be a treat for me to go out to the docks, if you would be my escort."

"Of course I will," Rebecca replied. "We could close the shop and take leave for at least one turn of the hourglass."

"Absolutely," Ruthie replied, patting Rebecca's hand.

"Then I shall take Maisey to the neck and keep my eye on the Sound," Mehti said. She turned and left the two women to continue their work.

The early morning was clear and sunny with a slight wind from the south. Maisey seemed pleased to be free of the wagon as they headed along the upper road to the neck of land that led to the beachhead she and Caleb used to frequent on their observation forays of the Sound. It was a three-mile ride, the roadway surrounded by mostly cleared land planted with head-high corn and potatoes yet to be harvested.

About halfway to her destination, Maisey started fidgeting when two cannon blasts, the signal to muster the militia, emanated from Long Island Sound. Mehti pulled Maisey up and dismounted, calming the horse.

"There, there—easy girl," Mehti soothed, stroking Maisey's neck.

Could it be New London was under attack? That made no sense to her. The Continental army was moving south, so why would the British be here in Connecticut? Frederic's last letter to Rebecca confirmed the army had traversed Philadelphia and were on their way to Yorktown. No sooner had these thoughts run through her mind than a distant third cannon blast sounded, signaling the all clear. Mehti breathed a sigh of relief and remounted her horse.

Within thirty minutes she arrived at the beach, dismounted, tied Maisey to some nearby brush and grabbed her spyglass.

She did not need to raise her spyglass to witnessed ships, many ships—British ships sailing straight for New London! At first she stood frozen in place, unable to breathe, stunned at what she was seeing. She lifted the glass and began to count, but there were so many, it was difficult to get a clear number. She thought perhaps there were more than twenty British vessels approaching.

Mehti's first thought was to get word to the town, but she was certain if she could view the vessels, the occupants of New London and Groton could see them, also. It occurred to her the third cannon blast must have been fired by the British, which meant the militia would not come to the defense of the towns. Her mind started racing, trying to figure out what she should do. Should she ride Maisey hard back to New London to warn Rebecca, Hut and the Cuthberts so they could flee for safety? She was sure Hut would stay and fight, but what of Rebecca and the Cuthberts?

The lead ships were hauling in their sails and lowering anchor as they simultaneously and swiftly lowered landing boats. The ships to the rear, headed toward the Groton side of the Thames, were doing likewise. She decided to observe the landing and get word back to town as to troop directions, the number of men landing and whether they were hauling cannon. She needed to move swiftly if she was going to be of any assistance. Mehti determined to ride as close as possible to the landing site, to observe the enemy, then race on ahead to New London to let the authorities know what to expect. Crossing nearby Alewife Cove at the mouth of the Thames would be too risky on horseback, so she decided to ride to the head of the cove and head east toward the stone lighthouse at Harris Point. From there she could observe the troops undetected from behind the stone walls nearby.

It took Mehti less than fifteen minutes to cross over the head of the brook-fed cove, make her way to the rise above the lighthouse and tie Maisey behind a tree. She crouched behind a stone wall; peering over, she had a clear view of White Beach, south of the lighthouse near Brown's farm, where several landing craft were approaching. To her surprise, two young militiamen came scurrying, hunched over, along the wall and crouched next to her.

"What are you doing here, missy?" the first one asked. "This is no place for a girl to be," he scolded.

"I wanted to try to count the men landing to warn the town," she responded.

"Word is already out," the man said. "We're certain there's too many of them to face head on. We're to try and kill or wound as many as we can when they head into town."

Several other men joined them, lined up behind the wall and waited for the landing party to come within range. Mehti peered over the wall with her spyglass and watched as several boats approached the beach. At the stern of one boat stood a man in a full blazing-red British uniform, brandishing a sword in one hand. He was shouting something to his men.

"Oh my! Is that who I think it is?" Mehti asked, then handed her spyglass to the militia man.

He peered through the glass. "That would be him, missy. That would be Benedict Arnold, that traitorous bastard! Excuse me, missy," he added realizing his tongue.

Mehti took the glass back from the man she suspected was a nearby farmer as even more men joined them. A shot rang out from one of the militiamen toward the landing party as they took their first steps onto the beach. Realizing their men risked being fired upon while they disembarked, two ships nearest the shore began cannon fire above the beach near where Mehti and the others were positioned. The boom of the blasts caused Mehti to cover her ears and shrink further behind the stone wall.

"I need to get into town," Mehti told the man stooping next to her.

"Keep your head down, missy," he yelled after her as she crouched, running to retrieve Maisey. The horse's nostrils flared and her eyes were wide with fear from the exchange of gunfire and cannon blasts. She wheeled around, panic stricken, and again Mehti tried to calm her, uncertain if she could even mount the horse, particularly as she was riding bareback. Maisey whinnied a shrill cry of fright, a sound Mehti had never heard from the animal before. She decided to untie the lead and draw the horse as far from the noise and commotion as possible before even attempting to mount her. As soon as the horse sensed its chance for freedom, she began to bolt, but Mehti held her tight. She ran alongside her for a ways until the horse began to slow and calm herself.

Mehti pulled Maisey toward a ledge outcrop on the side of the road and, stepping up on it, was able to mount the horse. Instantly Maisey flew into a gallop as the two headed north toward town along the high road that ran parallel to the river.

Chapter 24

I should stop first at Fort Nonsense. Mehti figured she could warn the men manning the fort that troops were disembarking. She could also get water for Maisey from the trough, then perhaps ride to the Shaw mansion and return the spyglass to Captain Shaw, who would surely need it.

Mehti had left the beachfront before all the landing boats had made their way to shore. But she had counted at least twenty boats headed for land, and estimated they each held thirty or more soldiers. Most were dressed in their red British uniforms, while others wore green uniforms with plumed head gear that she suspected were German Jaegers. But many were plain-clothed. In other words, they were Loyalists recruited for the mission. It sickened Mehti that fellow countrymen would take up arms against each other. But the country was truly divided. While Connecticut, Massachusetts and Rhode Island housed primarily Patriots, New York was a hotbed for Tories.

Fort Nonsense stood on Town Hill as an earthen work fort positioned uphill and west of Fort Trumbull, which lay on the waterfront. Mehti rode to within the walls of the fort, where approximately twenty men were already scurrying about to position their six cannons to be aimed at the approaching enemy a couple miles behind her.

William Eggers, a boy Mehti knew from the wharves, was perched on the branch of a tree that provided him with a view to the south.

Mehti shouted up to him. "What do you see from up there, William?"

William shaded his eyes and squinted. "I see two columns of soldiers heading north. One column is coming up the high road, headed straight for us. The other column is taking the shore road directly to town. There sure are a lot of them. Mehti, you should not be here," he added out of obvious concern as he began his descent. He jumped down from about six feet above and landed just in front of Mehti and Maisey.

"I've been down to Brown's farm and watched the British land. They've got cannons on their landing boats. And they are being led by Benedict Arnold!" Mehti exclaimed. "I think there are hundreds of them and I came to warn you."

"Oh, I can tell you we've had a very good look at the troops," he assured her. In the distance, volleys of musket fire crackled, along with continuous cannon fire from the ships.

"But there are so few men here! Surely you will not be staying here to defend this fort."

"We have no commander, so it's hard to say. I suspect we will hold them off as long as we can with these cannons, then spike the cannons and abandon last minute," the boy replied. He wheeled around to help push a cannon into place. As he helped get it set, he turned to her and yelled, "You need to leave now, Mehti! It's too dangerous. Head out of town with the others."

"Rebecca and Hut are at the Cuthberts'. I need to go find them. I also need to give Agent Shaw his spyglass. Maybe you should come with me. You're not safe here either, William."

"I can't leave now," he said. "But you go on. I'll leave with the men," he said with pride.

As Mehti exited the fort and headed into town, she looked to the south and saw many of the men who had been crouched beside her at the stone wall running up the road toward Fort Nonsense, trapped between fire from the enemy behind them and cannon fire now emanating from the fort in front of them that fell short. They waved their arms frantically to signal the fort to cease firing so they could make it there to safety.

Mehti walked Maisey toward town, going against a stream of frightened evacuees hurrying to leave before the British arrived. The escaping crowds included women pulling carts full of household items and children with sacks slung over their backs, stuffed with important papers or valuables. As the sound of musket fire grew louder and closer, a sense of panic began to consume the crowd.

A woman walked with four children following her, their eyes dazed with shock. The youngest quaked with fear as she clutched her corn doll to her chest. Mehti guessed she was no more than four or five years old.

"What about Father?" one boy asked the mother. He kept turning and looking behind him, searching the haphazard parade of people, and at one point turning to walk backward, straining to see through the crowd.

"Your father will stay behind to fight, Nathan. But we must head for the woods, so please come along," the mother scolded, her voice raised with tension.

Mehti continued toward Bank Street and past Bream Cove to the Shaw mansion. The town was a scene of chaos, particularly along the waterfront. Even the birds seemed to be flying in a frenzy, unsettled by the gun and cannon fire. From this vantage point, Mehti noticed several New London ships had already set sail and were heading upriver toward Norwich for safety. She wondered whether Hut were among them.

Arriving at Shaw Mansion, Mehti tied Maisey to the hitching post, grabbed the spyglass and strode up the granite stairs to the front door, knocking with urgency. The door slowly opened and a trembling Negress stared down at Mehti.

"Yes, miss?"

"Is Agent Shaw home? I need to return his spyglass to him. I'm certain he will need it."

"No, miss. Master Shaw went off fishing up the coast this morning. Thank the Lord, maybe he be safe," she said, wide eyed. "Me and the missus is heading out of town soon as we can," she added as she glanced around the room behind her in anticipation of their imminent departure.

"Please give this to your missus," Mehti said, handing the spyglass to the frightened woman. "God be with you," she added as she spun and headed back down the steps. It was now imperative she find Rebecca and Ruthie Cuthbert, who had planned to visit the wharves.

Chapter 25

Mehti paced up and down Bank Street in search of Rebecca and Mrs. Cuthbert. Men were busy gathering ammunition, loading muskets or boarding ships to head up the Thames River. She was pleased to see the *Josephine* was no longer at her slip. That could mean Hut was on board and heading upriver. With so much panic and commotion on the wharves, Mehti began to seriously doubt her sister and Ruthie were anywhere near.

Gunfire from British troops loomed closer and closer. To the south Mehti was shocked to see Fort Trumbull under attack. How had the British been able to move so quickly to make their way so far north? Once they took possession of Fort Trumbull, nothing would keep them from marching into New London as people now began streaming in the opposite direction out of town, taking Main Street to the north toward Quaker Hill. She had to make her way to the butcher shop and general store. If Rebecca, Ruthie and old man Cuthbert hadn't headed out of town, they could still be there, waiting for her. But in order to get to the Cuthberts', Mehti would have to head toward the advancing British troops.

Mehti stood at the head of a dock, trying to decide whether to join the flow of people heading north out of town, or to head west toward the shop. She chose west.

Within sight of the Shaw mansion, she saw Maisey, still tied to the hitching post where she'd left her, rearing up in panic at the sounds of musket shot and the throngs of people passing by. When Mehti was within twenty yards of her, Maisey reared her head and broke her tether. The horse careened into the roadway, heading north and swept right past Mehti, unstoppable. Mehti called out to her, but Maisey was so agitated, she paid no attention.

Mehti hiked up her skirt and ran as fast as she could to the butcher shop. She entered the shop, gasping for breath, and was relieved to see Rebecca, Ruthie and old man Cuthbert inside, gathering up belongings.

"Really, Robert, we must leave at once. There is nothing so important here that it is worth risking our lives," Ruthie chided.

Robert? Until this day Mehti had never heard anyone mention old man Cuthbert's given name was Robert. He was always addressed as Mr. Cuthbert, or referred to as old man Cuthbert.

"What about our silver? Do you want to leave that for those thieving bastards!" her husband replied. Turning to Mehti, he ordered, "Mehti, go upstairs to our room and bring down some socks from the chest. There should be at least four there." Then to Ruthie he said, "You take those socks and fill them with the silver coin I've stashed in the back of our medicine box. I'll get our ledgers. And we may need some food. Once we leave here, there's no telling when we'll be able to come back." He headed to the back of the store to the corner where his small desk stood, cluttered with papers.

"Where's Hut?" Mehti asked before ascending the stairs.

"He's out helping get our ships up river," Rebecca responded.

Ruthie was clearly distressed. On any given day, in spite of her lack of sight, she easily knew her way around the store. But in the commotion, she seemed disoriented, not sure what to do as she walked in circles, repeating over and over to her husband, "We must leave, Robert. We must leave!"

"Ruthie!" her husband yelled. "Calm yourself. I won't leave here until I have what we need. Now please, sit down."

"I'll grab a sack and start gathering some food from the shelves," Rebecca said, knowing old man Cuthbert meant what he said.

Mehti climbed the narrow stairs. Three doorways faced the hallway. She checked the first two and saw no chest; the third appeared to be the Cuthberts' bedchamber, with a chest up against the wall next to a wardrobe. She rummaged through bedding and clothing until she found three socks.

Mehti stepped to the window facing the harbor. Even though the shop stood a block away from the waterfront, from the second floor she had a clear view of the river below and Fort

Trumbull to the south. Smoke rose above the fort, and several men scurried to rowboats, to escape to Fort Griswold, directly across the river.

British and German Jaeger soldiers took aim from the banks of the earthen fort, capturing one boat while two others were able to escape. Mehti could not take her eyes away from the window as she watched the surreal events unfold. The British had taken Fort Trumbull less than a quarter of a mile away. She wondered what had become of Hut, and of Maisey.

Descending the stairs, she handed the socks to Ruthie, who deposited the silver coins, their life savings, into them.

"We only need two," Ruthie noted.

Rebecca filled two sacks with staples from the store—flour, sugar, oil, bread and cheese.

"Don't pack too much," Mehti told her. We need to be able to travel without too much weight.

"We have Maisey and the mule," Rebecca said.

"No, Becca, Maisey ran off. And the mule can't pull the cart alone. We can pack some items on him, but we'll need to walk out of town.

"Mehti, go around to the back and bring the mule through the alleyway and to the front of the store. We'll pack it there and head north with the others," Rebecca directed her sister.

From the back door of the store, Mehti passed through the butcher shop, where old man Cuthbert was rummaging through his desk. She stepped out to the pens behind the butcher shop, where the mule was circling, eyes bulging, nostrils flaring in panic.

"Easy, girl," Mehti said as she stepped into the muddy pen and tried to capture the agitated mule. The rope in her hand seemed to cause the mule even more fright, but she was able to corner the animal and slip the noose over its head to pull it from the pen. But the mule was not cooperating. Resisting her tug, it dug its hooves into the mud unwilling to yield. Realizing she was losing the battle, Mehti released the rope and walked over to the mule. She needed to take another tack.

"Easy, girl," Mehti repeated as she tried to stroke the mule's neck and flank. The mule's ears were laid back in consternation. Mehti tried to calm the animal even as the sounds of gunfire loomed closer and closer. But the animal would not settle down. Finally Mehti grabbed the rope, held tight and, with all her might, landed a blow on the rump of the mule—who lunged forward through the pen gate, with Mehti running alongside.

Inside the store, Rebecca and Ruthie were finished packing and ready to leave. As a precaution, Rebecca slid the two socks of silver coins under the skirt of her dress, concealing them within her pockets.

"Come, Ruthie, we must leave," she implored her friend as she lifted the woman by the forearm. "I'll carry one bag and then return for the other."

"I smell smoke," Ruthie exclaimed.

"It's from the gunfire," Rebecca told her.

"No! I smell smoke—wood smoke!" Ruthie said again, her voice rising. "I have to get Robert." She yelled to the back of the shop, her voice rising in fear, "Robert! We must go—Robert!"

There was no response. A crackling of fire now emanated from the back room. Ruthie began to cry as Rebecca led her toward the front door, one sack slung over her back.

"You have to go back for Robert!" Ruthie cried. "How did they get here so quickly?" she asked, expecting no answer.

The two women stepped out onto the stoop where Mehti was waiting with the mule.

"Can you get up on the mule?" Mehti asked Ruthie. "I can hoist you up." Ruthie felt for the mule's back and Mehti laced her fingers together to make a lift for the old lady, who was so slight she was easy to lift. Rebecca laid the first sack across the mule in front of Ruthie and was about to return to the house to find Mr. Cuthbert when two British soldiers patrolling the street came up to them, bayonets at the ready.

"What have we here?" one asked.

"We have two lovely ladies," the other sneered.

"And why are you in such a rush?" the first questioned. "You need not run off. We British can be quite accommodating, even to rebel wenches." The two of them began to laugh.

Rebecca found her tongue. "Please, I must go inside. There's a man in there and we need to get him out."

The soldier looked up at the building; flames had begun to consume the back of the structure.

"I doubt anyone is going to be coming out of that building," he scoffed, and again they laughed. "It makes no difference. We're going to burn this town to the ground – and all you rebels with it. But you two ladies don't have to leave quite so quickly."

Sensing grave danger for them all, Mehti, who held the rope to the mule's noose, leaned toward Ruthie and whispered, "Hold tight, Ruthie," and put the rope in her hands. She smacked the mule on the rump. The mule ran straight away down Bank Street, heading north, with Ruthie as its rider.

"I see we have a smart one here," the first soldier said, grabbing Mehti by the arm.

Just then another soldier approached and the two men immediately stood at attention.

"What goes on here?" he quizzed the two men.

"These two women were just trying to escape," the first soldier said.

"Then let them do so," their commander ordered. "Or are we fighting ladies now?" he added sarcastically.

Sensing the commander might help them, Rebecca spoke up. "Sir, there is a man trapped in this burning building and we need to get him out."

"If that is so, then that's one less rebel we need to fight," the commander replied. "Now be off with you!"

The soldier released his grip on Mehti and, as the two women quickly fled north out of town on foot, they saw British soldiers out on the wharves, setting fire to their ships. Even the *HMS Hannah*, New London's biggest prize capture by its privateers, was now aflame and drifting away from the end of its pier.

Chapter 26

As soon as Hut had heard a commotion on the street that morning, he wiped his hands on his apron and made his way out of the butcher shop and onto Bank Street. Looking to the south of the river, he gasped at the sight of several British vessels already weighing anchor or approaching the harbor. He hadn't made out the exact number of ships, but it was clear an attack on New London was imminent.

He had rushed back into the butcher shop, removed his apron and looked for old man Cuthbert, who was in the store.

"Sir, we is under attack. I's got to go," Hut told him hurriedly.

Without waiting for a reply, he ran out the back, toward the wharves and the *Josephine.* On his way, he passed Rebecca and Ruthie Cuthbert, who were headed back to the shop.

"You get on back to the shop," Hut had told them. "You be safe there."

They scurried along while Hut hastened to the ship.

When Hut arrived, Captain Treadwell was already there, preparing the ship to disembark. Three other crewmen, the minimum needed to set sail, assisted. Hut scampered up the rope ladder with one of his crewmates and out onto the yardarm to lower a sail. One sail would be enough to get them up the Thames with the same southerly breeze that brought the British to the mouth of the river. Fortunately, the *Josephine* was already positioned bow north at the end of the pier, and the tide was coming in, which was also to their advantage. Once the lanyards were released, the *Josephine* slowly navigated her way up the river with a few ships in front of her, and several others behind, attempting to leave New London.

Captain Treadwell waved Hut over to the wheel, motioning him to take charge of the vessel.

"Just don't run us aground," he told Hut, patting him on the shoulder. Treadwell headed to the stern of the ship with his spyglass to see if they were being followed; but no British vessels ensued. Cannon and musket fire was on the increase, a sign the battle in New London was worsening. When the *Josephine* reached as far as North Mamacoke, a peninsula sitting on the west side of the river, Treadwell could make out two rowboats crossing the Thames from Fort Trumbull to Fort Griswold, and he realized Fort Trumbull was being abandoned.

"May the British have mercy on the good citizens of New London," he said after hearing a large explosion issue from the heart of the city. Even without a spyglass, it was clear New London was burning, as smoke rose all along the waterfront. "Thank God we at least saved the *Josephine*," Treadwell said.

Hut looked back on New London and wondered what had become of Rebecca, Mehti and the Cuthberts.

He heard cannon and musket fire on the east side of the river at Fort Griswold. Just north of Mamacoke, Treadwell took over the wheel again and ordered the raising of the sails and lowering of the anchor.

"We have to go help," Hut said to the captain.

"There's not much we can do from here, Hut. And the winds are wrong for us to return probably until tomorrow."

Hut looked around nervously. He felt helpless, listening to the sounds of battle as he stood on the deck of the *Josephine*, unable to assist in any way.

"Is the rowboat on board?" Hut asked.

Treadwell shook his head. "There was no time, Hut. The rowboat is back at the dock, if there's even a dock left."

Looking over the side of the ship, Hut estimated the shore was about thirty yards away. While his swimming skills were rudimentary, he judged that he could swim ashore. He sat down on the deck and removed his boots. Then he grabbed a rope at the gunwales and lowered himself over the side and into the water, while Captain Treadwell and the rest of the crew watched from above. No one attempted to stop or follow him. Hut knew these men to be brave on the waters, but perhaps they saw themselves as seamen and not soldiers.

The river water was not terribly cold, it being September 6ᵗʰ and nearing the end of summer. Hut began by treading water and letting the incoming tide move him along while he paddled toward shore. He managed to grab hold of a protruding rocky outcrop in an area where there was no beach. He hoisted himself up on the rock, sat down to catch his breath, then waved to the men on the *Josephine.*

Hut knew a roadway ran north/south along the east side of the Thames from Groton village to the village of Gales Ferry. Between him and the roadway, he would need to pass through a mass of brambles in his bare feet – but he had endured much worse hardship in his trek north from Richmond, Virginia three years before.

Hut made his way through the thorny underbrush and came out at last on the road that followed the river, bordered by farmland to his left. He began his walk south toward Groton village and Fort Griswold. At one farm he passed by, he noticed an ox in the field, still hitched to the plow, where his owner left him in his haste to go and join the fight.

He saw no one on the road until a young boy came running in his direction, heading north, away from the fighting. His reddened cheeks were wet with tears, and Hut stopped him to see if he could help.

"I went to see," the boy cried, choking on his words. His shoulders quaked with each sobbing gasp of air. "I went to see," he repeated. "I never seen a battle before, so I went to see," the boy exclaimed.

"Where were you, boy?" Hut asked.

"I hid outside the fort, but I peered in. They run him through," he said and started crying uncontrollably again. Hut would have dried his tears, but all his clothes were still wet. He wiped the boy's tears away with his hand.

"Who run who through?" Hut asked.

"The British man in the red uniform. Colonel Ledyard surrendered his sword and the man run it right through him and killed him. And them men in red, they all started killing." He sobbed again, his chest heaving with each craggy breath.

Hut took a chance and hugged the boy to try to calm him down. Under normal circumstances, no black man would ever hug a white child who was a stranger to him. But these were not normal circumstances. "Was your daddy in the fort?" Hut asked.

"He was there, but I didn't see him. He told me to stay home, but I went to see. I don't know if he is dead or not," the boy sobbed. "They killed so many." The boy wiped his eyes with one sleeve, then his nose with the other.

Hut looked into the boy's eyes to make sure he had his attention. "Now you got to get back home and be brave for your mama. Promise you will do that." Hut said.

The boy slowly nodded his head up and down, suddenly grasping the responsibility of his mother's care. Then Hut released the boy and headed toward Fort Griswold along the river road.

"Don't go there, mister!" the boy called after him. "They will kill you if you go there." And then he ran up the road toward his farm.

Chapter 27

No sooner had Hut left the side of the young boy than the barrage of gunfire coming from Fort Griswold seemed to abate. An eerie silence followed. Hut picked up his pace, heading toward Groton village, which consisted of several homes and shops that sat along the banks on the east side of the river. As he neared the village, across the river he could see the carnage the British had wrought on New London.

Ships docked at the wharves were in flames. From this vantage point, Hut could see most of the town was also engulfed in flames. Plumes of heavy dark smoke billowing skyward obscured the sun, turning the day into night. Another huge explosion erupted, sending debris flying into the air. Again his thoughts turned to Mehti, Rebecca and the Cuthberts. Maybe he should have stayed with them, gotten them out of the city safely. But no one could have predicted the ruthlessness of the enemy.

Since it appeared the battle at Fort Griswold had ended, Hut wondered how he could help. He had come to fight, but now was uncertain how he could lend assistance. He decided to lie in wait from a safe distance somewhere along the shoreline. He moved from building to building, concealing himself and trying to get a view of the enemy's positions and activities.

Crouched in an alleyway by a fishmonger's shop, Hut had a clear view of the hillside leading up to the fort. The British were clearly in command. Along the waterfront below the fort, an officer was signaling one of their ships to bring transports to shore. Meanwhile, Hut could see both British and Patriot soldiers, wounded or dead, being carried out of the fort and laid side by side on the hill—the British placed in the shade of a large tree, the Patriots in the full sun. Just outside the fort, at the top of the hill, several wounded Americans were being loaded onto a wagon to transport them to the boats waiting below. But the overloaded wagon became too heavy for the British soldiers to control. When they lost their grip, the wagon careened down the hill and struck a tree stump. The impact tossed the men about like netted fish. Their wails of agony jettisoned across the hill. Hut felt helpless to do anything to assist them.

Those who were able to walk were marched to the base of the hill and told to sit in wait of their transport. They would be prisoners of war, left to rot in prison ships or – hopefully – be traded for British prisoners.

Hut stepped back further into the alleyway when soldiers bearing torches came down the road, intent on setting fire to the homes and shops along the waterfront. He decided his best course of action would be to leave, lest he be trapped between burning buildings, or discovered by the British.

As he stood to leave his hiding place, he felt a jab in his back.

"What do we have here? A blackie!" a British soldier said from behind him.

"Turn around, blackie!"

Hut slowly turned around to view the grinning face of the enemy. For a moment, he thought he could grab the soldier's bayonet and overpower him, since the man was easily a foot shorter than Hut and very slight, hidden in his uniform. But a torch-wielding solder joined them and Hut knew he was outnumbered. If he were closer to the river, he might have been able to jump in and possibly swim to safety, but the river was easily two rods away.

"Look at this one, will you, Henry? A coward hiding in an alleyway while his fellow soldiers risk their lives. Put your hands on your head!" the soldier ordered as he nudged Hut with the bayonet. He motioned Hut out onto the roadway and pushed him toward the shoreline, where prisoners were being told to sit on the bank to await transport to a British vessel.

Hut sat in the sun with about thirty other men for almost two hours, surrounded and guarded by several sentries, while the British collected their wounded and buried their dead. Hut looked around him at the other prisoners and realized he didn't know any of the men being held. When the transport boats finally arrived, the prisoners were ordered to form into two columns; twelve at a time were marched, six to a side, knee deep into the water, where they were told to get on board.

The prisoners were rowed out into the river and positioned alongside a ship anchored off shore. One by one, they were told to climb topside while British soldiers waited above, their bayonets at the ready. A quick walk to the hatch and the men were paraded down to the hold, choking from the smoke of the fire burning at its center, maintained for cooking. As soon as all the men were secured in the hold, the hatch was closed, so there was a total lack of ventilation to give relief from the oppressive heat and stifling smoke.

Hut considered himself fortunate. Although his discomfort was considerable, he was uninjured, unlike so many of the men brought below. In spite of their battle loss and the extent of their injuries, the men began immediately discussing plans for taking over the ship.

Chapter 28

Ruthie had never ridden on a mule in her life. While she was grateful to have been able to escape New London, she now had no idea where she was and felt frightened for herself and for the likelihood that Robert might not have survived the attack. She also had no idea what had happened to Mehti and Rebecca. When her fears overcame her, her bottom lip would begin to quiver, but she refused to cry. Then she would take a deep breath and try to keep control of herself. *All is not lost,* she told herself over and over.

The security Ruthie felt in her life came from her knowledge of her familiar home and store, a place where she knew every counted step to the things she needed to live her life. Now she was totally at the mercy of the unknown. She had no idea where she was. As she and the mule exited the city, she viewed only shadows of people passing by her. And she heard the panic and uncertainty in their voices as they fled alongside her.

Fortunately for her, the mule knew exactly where it was, which was on the road toward Norwich, the road it had taken every time its owners traveled from New London to Granville. After being hit on the rump by Mehti, it took almost twenty minutes for the mule to slow its pace on the outskirts of the town, away from the noise and commotion caused by the attack. Then it slowed to a saunter, its head down as usual, on its way back home, traveling up through the hills of Quaker Hill. Ruthie could sense the change in grade when she leaned into the animal as it headed up the familiar slopes.

Along the way, Ruthie could hear groups of men on horseback talking about whether to enter the city or hold back because of their concern they would be outnumbered. She didn't recognize anyone's voice and assumed they were militiamen from farms north of New London, or perhaps from Norwich. And nobody took any notice of an old blind woman riding by on a mule.

Finally the din of noise and commotion was behind her and she decided to dismount to rest the mule and give her backside a rest as well. She swung her leg around and slid down, making sure to keep hold of the mule's rope. Then, bending down, she felt the ground beneath them—dirt. She moved to the side, hoping to find some grasses for the mule, and also to provide a place for herself to sit and rest. Finally, after some trial and error, she identified at least a patch of grasses to sit on.

The cooling of the air told Ruthie it must be late afternoon or early evening. That gave her another concern. Where would she spend the night? Surely she couldn't just lie by the side of the road. Her bottom lip began to quiver again, but she brought it to a halt once more. *All is not lost—I will not lose hope.* The hope Ruthie felt was that Rebecca and Mehti were safe and would be following along behind her at some point, and that all would be well.

Ruthie heard approaching footsteps on the roadway. It sounded like more than one person.

"Ruthie Cuthbert, is that you?" a recognizable voice called out to her.

It was Mrs. Potters approaching, and it sounded like her children were with her children. The woman visited the Cuthberts' store on a weekly basis and Ruthie would recognize her voice anywhere.

"Oh, Mrs. Potters, what a relief to hear a familiar voice!"

"What are you doing out here all by yourself? Where is Mr. Cuthbert?" Mrs. Potters asked.

"I wish I knew. We were separated during the attack and I have had no contact with him since leaving New London. I know not his condition. And you remember Rebecca Tewkesbury who frequently helps me at the store. She was there with me when the British attacked and I fear for her and her sister as well. And what of Isaiah?"

"He ran to Fort Nonsense this morning with his musket in his hand and I haven't heard from him since. When he left, he instructed us to leave the house if a threat was imminent, take our important papers and to give no quarter. When the men came through the town, the children and I were sitting down for a meal. But I was so fearful, we had to leave. I suspect the invaders enjoyed our stew before burning our home. We are on our way to my sister's farm in Montville Parish. She will bring me back once we receive the all clear," the woman said. "You must come with us, Mrs. Cuthbert. If you stay by the side of the road, I fear it will be at your peril."

"Excuse me, Mrs. Potters, but where exactly am I?"

"You are on the Norwich Road, about three miles from Montville Parish."

Ruthie mulled over the offer. "I feel I must stay here, Mrs. Potters. I have faith that if I wait here, on the main road, I will be found by Rebecca Tewkesbury, who will surely be on her way just behind me, only on foot without benefit of a mule. If I were to go home with you, we should not connect. No, I appreciate your kindness, but I must say here," Ruthie replied. She reached out her hand. "Please take my hand," Ruthie told the woman.

Mrs. Potters bent down and did as she was asked. Ruthie held the woman's hand to her cheek, then kissed the back of it before releasing it. "You are an angel, Mrs. Potters, but I will be fine here. I must wait, you see."

"You have faith, I can see that. I have faith also—faith that my husband will return to me." Then she paused, as if in thought. "Very well, Ruthie Cuthbert. You are a stubborn blind woman if ever there was one, and we will menace you no more."

With that, Mrs. Potters and her children moved on, in hopes of covering the few remaining miles in time to share a meal with her sister.

Again the roadway became quiet and all Ruthie could hear was the sound of the mule munching on grass. She wasn't sure how long she sat there before she heard footfalls again on the road. This time it sounded like one person with a tendency to drag his feet. She thought perhaps it was a wounded person unable to carry his weight due to the injury. What if it was a British soldier who had decided to desert? All manner of frightening thoughts ran through Ruthie's head and she began to feel a sense of panic. She'd made a mistake. She should have gone with Mrs. Potters.

The distinct smell of wood smoke entered the perimeter of her senses and the traveler stopped directly in front of her. She sat perfectly still when the intruder sat down beside her.

"Ruthie my bride, you are a sight for sore eyes!" Robert exclaimed. "And that there mule is a godsend."

"Robert!" Ruthie exclaimed, overcome with relief. "How did you ever get out of the shop? I thought you were dead for sure!"

"Snuck out the back just in time," Robert told her. "But the shop and the store, they're gone, Ruthie. We've not got a thing left to our name, except this sack of paperwork," he said, patting the sack he had crammed with his ledgers.

"Did you see Rebecca and Mehti along the way?"

"No sign of them, I am sorry to say."

Finally feeling safe, Ruthie began to cry. "What do we do now, Robert?" she asked, her voice weary.

Robert was not accustomed to outwardly showing affection to the wife he loved more than anything in the world. He took her hand and held it tight. "I don't know, Ruthie. Right now, I just need to set a spell, rest my bones and thank the Lord we are alive. There are many today I fear who have not fared as well as we have."

Chapter 29

Rebecca and Mehti made their way through the streets of New London, trying to determine their safest course. So many people were exiting the town to the north, they decided to move along with the throngs who became more frightened as the sounds of battle grew closer.

As they passed onto Main Street, they could see the *HMS Hannah* being set on fire at its pier by British soldiers.

"How foolish that they would burn their own ship," Mehti exclaimed.

"Better it be burned, I suppose, than be left in the hands of Patriots," Rebecca said.

"If we could only find Maisey, this would be so much easier."

In a short distance they came upon the warehouse holding the spoils of the *Hannah*. A flurry of activity ensued with approximately twenty to thirty local men entering and exiting the wide-open warehouse doors, the booty in their hands. As the women looked on in surprise, one passing man said, "No sense leaving this all to the British, now is there?" And off he fled, a bolt of fabric over his shoulder.

Mehti and Rebecca followed along with maybe a hundred residents vacating the town with their parcels in tow. Children aged around eight or ten years of age walked along alone, no parent at their sides. One woman had balanced a straw mattress on the back of a goat that she pulled by a tether. A boy passed them balancing a yoke across his shoulders, from which hung cauldrons and cooking utensils. A man ahead of them carried an infant-sized casket, the one precious item he dared not leave behind.

Then, from behind the throngs of town folk, a man shouted, "They're right behind us! The British are right behind us," which set off a panic among the crowd. People began dropping their parcels and running to save themselves. The man with the casket, realizing he could not move swiftly with his precious package, made his way into the nearby burial ground, removed his child from the casket, determined to bury it. He dug feverishly until the hole was large enough to accommodate the wrapped infant. Laying the child inside, he covered it over and marked the location with a large stone.

Joining the moving throng, he strode alongside Mehti, who glanced in his direction and noted the man's solemnity. "He died yesterday," the man told her, reading her thoughts. "My wife the day before—smallpox."

Mehti just nodded in understanding.

"A proper burial will take place if and when we are able to return," he added almost apologetically.

As they left the town, the people of New London scattered in different directions, heading for the woods and surrounding hills for safety. Recurring explosions caused the crowd to cry out in alarm, as a general state of frenzy enveloped the evacuating masses. Mehti and Rebecca chose to keep to the Norwich Road, as they had always done when leaving the town.

On a hill outside of town, they came upon the same group of militiamen Ruthie had passed, their leader, spyglass in hand, viewing the carnage taking place. They were still engaged in discussion about which course of action they should take, but again appeared to opt for holding themselves to a safe distance, concerned they would be outnumbered in any enemy engagement, which was, of course, true.

Rebecca and Mehti passed them by and continued on their walk along the Norwich Road. Once they passed the militiamen, they slowed, certain they were out of immediate danger. They continued on in silence, both of them pondering the events of the day, wondering what had become of Ruthie, old man Cuthbert and Hut.

About a mile outside of town, in a field of grasses, they spied Maisey off in the distance, grazing. Mehti was so relieved to see her horse – to know no one had taken her and she appeared unharmed. Mehti called out to the mare, who immediately recognized her call, lifting her head and rotating her ears. A second call brought Maisey limping across the field to greet her owner with a gentle nuzzle.

"Good girl, Maisey," Mehti said, petting the horse's muzzle and withers. Then she reached down and felt Maisey's front right cannon.

"I don't feel anything broken. Maybe it's a sprain. But we'll have to walk her home," Mehti told her sister. "We don't dare ride her in this condition."

Mehti took Maisey's bridle and they headed north up the Norwich Road. Rebecca guessed it was now late afternoon and they were only a few miles outside New London. She began to give some thought to how they might spend the night when up ahead they spotted two people sitting along the side of the road with an animal nearby. As they got closer, Rebecca thought she would burst with joy to realize that who and what they saw in the distance were Ruthie, old man Cuthbert and their mule.

Rebecca waved to old man Cuthbert, who immediately let Ruthie know who was heading toward them. When they finally reached the Cuthberts, it was a tender reunion, all of them so grateful to have safely weathered the events of the day.

"I am so relieved to see that you are safe," Rebecca told Ruthie. "But how did you know the way?"

"Oh, the mule knew the way," Ruthie said with a smile.

"And where is Hut? Have you seen Hut?" Mehti asked.

"Hut left the shop as soon as he realized the British were in the harbor. He said he was going to help get the *Josephine* upriver – at least that is what he said to me before he ran out the back door," old man Cuthbert said.

Their joyous moment turned to one of quiet concern as they all looked to the south, in the expectation of seeing Hut coming up the road as they all had done.

"Well, Hut can take care of himself," Mehti said.

Rebecca nodded in agreement.

"What shall we do now?" Ruthie asked. "Our shop has evidently been destroyed by fire. We have lost everything."

"Oh, you must come and stay with us, Ruthie," Rebecca said. "You and Robert can have Father's room. I am sure Jacob will approve. And there's a farm about a mile north of here where hopefully we can stay for the night, even if it's in the barn," she added.

The four began their trek north, but took a moment to look to the south once more to see billows of smoke high in the air over what was New London.

Chapter 30

Just as Rebecca had expected, Jacob had no concern about giving the Cuthberts Gabriel's bedchamber.

"You may stay as long as necessary," Jacob told old man Cuthbert.

"I can be helpful," the old man replied with pride. "I can work the fields and help with the harvest. I can milk the cow, draw water and do patches and repairs about the house. And Ruthie and I, we keep to ourselves, so we won't be an intrusion."

"We have room, and we have plenty here," Jacob replied, patting old man Cuthbert on the back.

So it was for so many people who lost their homes in both New London and along the banks of Groton Village. Farm families on the outskirts of both devastated areas opened their hearts and their doors to provide shelter and food to those who had lost their homes and the harvested food stores they had put aside for winter—now all destroyed.

As news filtered to the outlying towns, it became clear that the biggest tragedy was the unnecessary loss of life. The majority of Americans in the Fort Griswold battle were killed post-surrender, in a few moments of frenzied killing, most tragic among them the murder of Colonel William Ledyard, run through with his own sword. Ledyard was the father of seven children, the youngest only ten days old. When word came the morning of the invasion, his wife—with their new infant—was put on a barge and sent up river to safety, never to see her husband again.

The saddest story was about the Perkins family. The morning of the attack, dedicated Patriots, the Perkinses answered the call, and paid the supreme price of losing not one, but six members of their family. Many widows were made from the battle at Fort Griswold. And many children lost their fathers that day—so many faced destitution.

The report on the loss of Patriot lives varied, depending on who spread the news. Some said 89, others said 93. Either way, it was a devastating number for so small a community. And nobody understood why New London was invaded, since the war effort had shifted to the south. It was still difficult to know about the loss of property. Again, reports varied.

"Over a hundred buildings burned to the ground, and a hundred families without homes," said one man at White Horse Tavern.

"Retaliation!" others cried. "We privateers got under the skin of those Redcoats, plain and simple."

Among the buildings burned were not only homes, but warehouses, the jail, courthouse and the Episcopal Church that had rung bells of celebration when privateers captured the *HMS Hannah* months before.

The day after everyone's return to the White farm, at their first full meal together, Jacob led the grace.

"Dear Lord, we beseech you to give comfort to those who are suffering, to take into your heavenly gates those who have passed and surely have earned celestial glory, to please keep watch over Hut, wherever he may be; and may the devil take the soul of Benedict Arnold at his earliest convenience. Amen."

"I don't know that your prayer is very Christian, Jacob," Rebecca scolded her brother.

"Perhaps, but I do not believe that man is a child of God, so I took liberties. And I use the term 'man' with great reservation, as I believe him to be little more than a treasonous coward," Jacob replied with contempt.

Ruby bent over and kissed the forehead of her son, Malcolm. "Don't you worry none, Malcolm. Your daddy be back, yes he will." Then she looked around the room for affirmation from the family.

"Yes, he will," Mehti added with conviction, smiling at Ruby. And she believed it to be true.

"There is some good news," Rebecca said. And she reached into her pockets and pulled out the two socks of silver coin she had stowed when they left New London.

"Oh, my!" old man Cuthbert exclaimed.

"What is it?" Ruthie asked.

"Rebecca saved our silver coins," her husband told her. "We can start over," he said, taking his wife's hand.

So much news was being spread across the county, particularly about the traitor, Arnold. He was rumored to have dined at the home of an old friend before having the house torched. Some said they witnessed him standing at the base of the burying ground, spyglass in hand, a good vantage point to view the slaughter taking place across the river at Fort Griswold. His conduct is what caused him to be hated by all Patriots.

The next morning, Jacob and old man Cuthbert borrowed two horses and rode to New London to survey the carnage that had been reported. The devastation left them speechless as they wandered through the rubble.

Others milled about the town, trying to salvage what they could of their belongings. Some sections remained unscathed; along Bradley Street, known as Widows' Alley, many houses still stood. Nathaniel and Lucretia Shaw's mansion sustained some fire damage, but was habitable. For the most part, the rest of New London was a pile of rubble and ashes, as was the case with the Cuthberts' store and butcher shop. Nothing remained. Jacob searched for their wagon, which had been left behind the store, but there was no sign of it, so he assumed it had either been consumed by the flames or someone had confiscated it. He stood on the site, scratching his head, realizing how hard it must be for old man Cuthbert to see all his property destroyed, knowing all *he* had to do was build another wagon.

Chapter 31

"Please," one prisoner cried out to a sentry who briefly opened the hatch. "We are suffocating. A breath of air, or if you intend to kill us, do it now and spare our misery."

"Please spare us," another man cried out, certain he would be put to death at any moment. But in the middle of the night, a brief respite surfaced as the British sentries opened the hatch and allowed two prisoners at a time to go up on deck, the Brits' bayonets always at the ready. Each pair of men was allowed two tours of the deck, then deposited back to the hold of the sloop. Hut went topside last. He breathed deeply, not knowing if it would be his last.

The prisoners went without food or water for about a day and then were served hogs' brains from captures the British had made while in Groton. The food was barely palatable, but Hut was grateful, for he knew it would sustain him. Finally the prisoners were afforded water. This pattern of existence continued for four more days as the sloop made its way down Long Island Sound, headed for New York.

Hut wasn't sure how it happened, but the sentries perhaps overhead the prisoners talking about commandeering the ship, and topside privileges were revoked.

On the fifth day, the hatch was opened and a British sentry yelled down, "Time for new quarters, you rebels!" The men looked about apprehensively, uncertain of their fate.

"Let's go, move along. I want two of you up here on deck," the sentry yelled down. And two by two, the men exited the hold. As the first two prisoners went topside, Hut listened for gunfire, wondering if execution was the Brits' intention. When the next set of men was ordered topside, he breathed a sigh of relief. Again, he was last to exit the hold.

When Hut arrived on deck, there were no other prisoners there. "Put your hands behind your back!" a sentry ordered while another stood by, his bayonet leveled at Hut's chest.

His hands were bound tightly.

"Over the side with you!" the sentry yelled, shoving Hut toward the gunwales.

Hut saw that a transport had been pulled alongside the ship and other prisoners were already on board. In the distance he saw a British brig and determined it was their intended destination. He scanned the horizon to see if he recognized any land mass, but nothing looked familiar.

Uncertain how best to exit the sloop with his hands behind his back, Hut jumped feet first and landed on his side, on the floor of the transport.

"Keep put right there!" a sentry ordered. Hut dared not move.

After a brief row to the brig, the prisoners were heaved up and over the bulwarks, onto the deck. All were lined up, and ordered to stay in line, one guard per prisoner, bayonets drawn. Again, Hut feared execution. To add to their misery, heavy rain began to fall and the men were left standing for two hours, after which they were allowed to lie on the deck, their hands still bound behind them.

Eventually the prisoners were allowed into the hold, where they remained for four days with barely any food or water. Any talk of mutiny had vanished. Hut mostly kept to himself. Since so much time had passed, talk turned to speculation that either they would be held indefinitely or used for a prisoner exchange. Hut counted thirty American prisoners on board.

"Did any of you men see de British taken prisoner?" Hut asked a group of men sitting below deck next to him.

"Any prisoners would have been taken in New London," one man answered. "There were no British captives at Fort Griswold. Just us and the dead or dying."

Two days later, the men were moved to yet another ship, the prison ship *Jersey*. Hut seemed to remember Rebecca telling him her husband, Oliver, had once been a prisoner on this very ship, but managed to escape and swim to shore. Hut had never seen such horrific conditions for human beings in his lifetime as in this hold—even during his slave days. The men were emaciated, most with just rags covering their bodies. Hut again considered himself lucky as he tried not to stare at other prisoners either propped up against outside walls of the hold or lying down—some in their own feces—so weakened they were unable to walk. The stench was unbearable. Until now, the prisoners from Fort Griswold had been separate, but on the *Jersey* they all became part of a larger prison population—easily forgettable among the masses. *I could die here,* Hut thought.

He estimated there were some two hundred men crammed into the hold of the *Jersey.* The only thing that drove fear from his heart were his thoughts of Ruby and his son, Malcolm. He would close his eyes and envision the White farm in Granville, Ruby sitting on the front stoop, Malcolm, almost one year old now, navigating the tall grass.

On their third day aboard the *Jersey,* a British soldier descended the hatch ladder with a man behind him, whom Hut did not recognize.

"Which ones are you wanting to take?" the soldier said.

The man immediately pulled out a kerchief and held it to his nose, then scanned the hold. He pointed to several of the men taken from Fort Griswold. The soldier motioned for each prisoner to exit the hold and make his way up the hatch ladder. Hut realized the man did not know who he was, and felt sure he would be overlooked. As the man pointed to the prisoner next to Hut, the prisoner stood then turned and motioning to Hut said, "This man as well."

The man doing the choosing stepped over to Hut and ordered him to stand. Looking him up and down, he said to Hut, "You too."

Hut jumped to his feet and made his way to the ladder. He had started to scamper up when he paused and looked around at the men who would be left behind for a certain death. He made his way up the ladder and took a deep breath of fresh air. He and the other men were lowered onto the deck of Nathaniel Shaw's private ship, the *Queen of France*. Hut learned later that Ebenezer Ledyard and Nathaniel Shaw had been designated as "Flag Officers" to negotiate a trade of prisoners. On board the ship, the prisoners, now no longer captive, were having their wounds tended to, and given water and sustenance.

Grateful for his rescue, Hut made his way to the bow of the ship, got down on his knees and prayed. "Dear God, I don't know why I should be free, but I thank you for watching over me. Ruby and Malcolm, I's sure they thank you, too. I will repay this blessing every day of my life with good deeds that will make you proud." He wiped the tears from his face as he stood. The turn of events was inconceivable to him, but it would only be a matter of time now before he was home.

Chapter 32

It had been over a month since the attack on New London and Groton. Ruthie and Robert Cuthbert had settled into the household as if they had always lived there, and Rebecca found Ruthie's companionship comforting. The two women had bonded well during Rebecca's trips to New London, and now that they were living together, the bond grew even deeper.

As September turned to October and the harvest began to dwindle, word of the devastation caused by the invasion continued to reach Granville. Jacob and Jon Bear frequented the White Horse Tavern for the latest news, then shared what they had learned at the dinner table, usually late in the evening after the day's field work was complete. The nights were turning chilly, even with October's warm days, and Jacob feared for friends displaced by the battle.

"At the tavern, they posted a flyer with the most recent numbers on our losses," Jacob said as he looked around the table at the faces of his loved ones. "It startles me to hear such numbers. But hardest of all is learning of the condition of so many widows and orphans. More must be done to help them. Fortunately, outlying families are still providing refuge—and will probably continue to do so through the winter months." He looked around the table and noticed everyone had stopped eating, listening intently.

"The report of a hundred forty-three buildings destroyed is on both sides of the river seems an accurate count. During Nathaniel Shaw's trip to Whitestone to exchange prisoners, he heard the British lost two hundred twenty men. I daresay that's a considerable number. They tossed overboard their wounded who died aboard ship. They've been washing up on shore at General Neck, evidence of that truth."

"I have not been there, and I shan't go, either," Mehti said with conviction. "The thought of Caleb drowning at sea, then going to General Neck and seeing bodies on shore—I cannot—and will not—go there anymore.

"I don't know if I even want to speak of Arnold. How evil can a person become, I ask? They say he commanded his men to do their duty to burn the town. They say he stood at the heights of the cemetery by Winthrop's tomb to purview the destruction from that vantage point. They say he dined with Loyalists James Tilly and Jeremiah Miller at Tilly's home on Bank Street before the house caught fire and they all managed to escape its burning. It turns out both their homes were burned to the ground. I see justice in that outcome. What kind of human being would enact such heinous deeds? An evil human I say—evil to his core."

"May he burn in hell!" Robert Cuthbert exclaimed.

The family again grew silent, no objection voiced. Finally, old man Cuthbert broke the silence.

"I'm planning on rebuilding," old man Cuthbert said. "But there's no seasoned lumber now. Maybe in the spring."

Ruthie patted his hand in support. "We shall overcome," she said.

"Now that the harvest is over, Hut, Jon Bear and I will start felling trees this week," Jacob said. "The saw mill is going to be too busy, so we'll be hand sawing. The wood can season over winter and we can plan on building in the spring. But we'll need a wagon to transport the wood."

"A wagon sure would help," Jon Bear said.

"I've been weaving," Ruby said. "I gots a couple of fine blankets we could trade with the wheelwright in Norwich. If'n we could get some wheels made, Hut could make us a wagon in a couple of days," she suggested.

"Shore could," Hut said.

Jacob looked around the table and reflected on their circumstances, grateful they were all alive and well. He had grown up in this house with his mother, father and sisters, with Jon Bear always nearby. Now their family consisted of an Indian, two former slaves and their son, elderly neighbors—the Cuthberts—his sisters and nephew, Oliver. And yet they had become a functioning family out of necessity and mutual caring.

He glanced at his wife, Rachael, and noticed she was not eating. This pregnancy caused her much sickness compared to her pregnancy carrying Abigail. He could tell she had lost weight when she should have been gaining.

"You must eat, Rachael," he said out of concern. She nodded but spoke not a word.

Usually after dinner, the women and children would walk along the green, but the sun had already set and a chill had come on with an accompanying wind. They all opted to sit in the parlor by the fireplace, the men lighting their pipes, the women setting to their needlework. The room was quiet, now that the children had been put to their beds.

"Oh, I just remembered," Jacob said, looking over at Rebecca. He walked to his desk and retrieved an envelope. "From Frederic Dubois," he said handing her the letter.

Rebecca flushed for a moment, overcome with guilt. Admittedly, she had not given much thought to Frederic since the invasion, so much had been happening since that fateful September 6th. Her mind had been consumed with the welfare of family and friends and the settling in of the Cuthberts. She thought she would rather read her letter in the privacy of her bedchamber, but the fire so warmed her she decided to read it to herself immediately, aware of her family's watchful eyes. She opened the letter, surprised by its relatively recent date.

September 25, 1781

My dearest Rebecca –

I write to you in haste, what may be my last correspondence. We received word of the invasion of New London and I pray you were not in the town at the time. I am almost delirious with worry as I have not received any correspondence from you.

Our march south has been grueling with more insects and heat. Tomorrow we march for Gloucester, Virginia under orders of General Washington. There we anticipate encountering the enemy as it is our understanding that Tarleton and the British hold the ground there. The main American and French army marches on to Yorktown.

I pray that I will live to see you again, sweet Rebecca. I would be strengthened in this battle if only I knew you to be well.

Word has come to us that Lafayette advises we "remember New London" as we face our impending fight. But most of all, I shall think of you, my dearest.

With utmost affection,

Frederic

Rebecca set the letter down on her lap, then gently brushed her fingers across the script, as if to feel Frederic's presence.

Jacob studied her face. "He is well?"

"I only wish I knew," she replied, knowing the letter was almost three weeks old.

Chapter 33

One would have expected that early October would bring some relief from the heat of summer, but the ride toward Gloucester Point had been in stifling heat, the hottest of days experienced thus far by the American and French armies as they marched south.

George Washington and the Continental army, along with Rochambeau, the Marquis de Lafayette and the French army, traveled the twelve short miles from Williamsburg to Yorktown. Meanwhile, Washington dispatched the Duc de Lauzun's Hussars to join the Virginia militia to secure Gloucester Point across from Yorktown—dispelling any thoughts of a British escape from Yorktown across the York River.

Frederic and his fellow Hussars were travel weary, but the anticipation of finally engaging the enemy caused a pitch of anticipation that stimulated the senses. As the hundreds of cavalry men headed southwest toward Gloucester Point, the countryside, flat as a griddle, displayed growth from a fertile soil that had produced a valuable tobacco crop for more than a century. Like so much of the South, the area appeared vacant—abandoned homes with doors hanging on their hinges and windows smashed. The otherwise-fertile fields lay fallow, the road grasses high. It was clear the British had been foraging throughout the area, supplying their troops. All the more reason for the French and American armies to secure the location.

"We anticipate that Tarleton is holding the Point," Frederic said to his tent mate, Armand, who rode alongside him.

"Yes, I have heard that as well. And I have my sword to greet him."

"That would be a fortunate day for either one of us," Frederic said, laughing.

"Did you manage to write to your mademoiselle before we embarked?" Armand asked.

"Rebecca? Yes, but so briefly."

"You are a fortunate man to have someone waiting for you, Frederic."

"And what of you, Armand? Do you have no one waiting for your return?"

"Only my mother," the Frenchman replied, laughing. "Right now she seems a million miles away."

At mid-morning, the caravan of soldiers stopped at Seawell's Tavern, about three miles from Gloucester Point, to rest and meet up with additional Virginia militiamen. Lauzun entered the tavern to meet with other officers while the men littered the nearby fields and the cavalry watered their horses. Frederic's chestnut stallion, which had been well fed and groomed throughout the march south, seemed a bit jittery, as if it anticipated an impending battle. *Perhaps he can smell something in the air,* Frederic thought as he stroked the horse's muzzle.

Frederic watched as all the officers exited the tavern.

Lauzun walked toward his men. "We march toward the British fortress at Gloucester Point," he said. "The cavalry shall lead."

And with that, Frederic and his Hussar comrades mounted their steeds as the men in the fields grabbed their muskets and formed columns, four men across. In total, there were 2,900 allied forces ready to grapple with the British. Frederic suspected every American and French soldier there had but one person on their mind—and that was the hated and dreaded Banastre Tarleton, so ruthless a British soldier.

The Great Road, as it was called, to Gloucester Point was shrouded with trees on either side. In the distance Frederic could see, from the prominence of light entering the forest, a clearing must be at hand. Lauzun, at the head of the column, entered the clearing first and, purveying the grounds, immediately saw a contingent of British on horseback at the far end of the field, emerging from the woodlands, perhaps out on a foraging expedition. Lauzun wasted no time in deciding his next maneuver. Within his sights he immediately recognized Banastre Tarleton leading a contingent of British cavalry.

"Charge!" he yelled to the men as he raised his pistol, aimed directly at Tarleton. The cavalry trailed Lauzun, racing their horses across the field to engage the British. The Hussars were laden with both spears and swords, and Frederic raised his sword, his first weapon of choice, dug his heels into his steed's sides and lurched forward.

The British seemed to be caught unawares, but no sooner had the Hussars entered the clearing than the British cavalry positioned themselves to return the charge. The adversaries met at mid field, where dust billowed and shots began to ring out.

Frederic made a first pass, leaning to the right and wielding his sword toward the neck of a passing cavalryman. But his reach fell short, grazing instead the soldier's shoulder. Frederic swiftly brought his horse around and engaged another soldier, fencing with the Brit, who lost his balance and fell to the ground. Frederic reared his horse in an attempt to trample the enemy, but the soldier rolled out of the way and ran off through the dusty foray, heading for the bordering woodlands.

From the corner of his eye, Frederic could see Tarleton on his horse, engaged in battle. A spear shot across an opening aimed at a rider, but missed its mark and struck a horse, felling both rider and animal. They careened into Tarleton's horse and he was lain upon the ground.

Swiftly a comrade rode to Tarleton's rescue, hoisting him onto the back of his horse as Tarleton ordered a retreat to the woods. The Hussars regrouped as the French and American infantry entered the field. Tarleton remounted and ordered a charge. Again shots rang out and a bullet whizzed past Frederic's head. He charged forward and again raised his sword to encounter the enemy. Passing him by, he wheeled his horse around to re-engage. Then the order came from Lauzun for the Hussars to exit to the left and right, to allow the infantry to take the field. Marching forward, their muskets raised, the joint French and Virginia infantry pushed back the British to the woods again, this time wounding Tarleton, who was lifted off the field by his men and taken to safety.

At that point, the battle seemed to turn in the Americans' favor, the British attempting one more time to reconnoiter and charge the field. But they were held back by the infantry. The sounds of gunfire and sword clanks dominated the field. Dust and musket smoke filled the air. Frederic raised his sword and re-entered the field, feeling confident that victory was beckoning, when a bullet struck him in his side. A piercing pain shooting through his body. He slumped forward, laying his torso upon the neck of his horse, trying desperately to maintain his balance. Frederic managed to turn his horse around in an attempt to head back behind lines, but he could not maintain his mount. As he fell to the ground, his horse ran off.

Frederic lay on his back, staring up at the sky. He closed his eyes and realized he was unable to move. He opened his eyes again, straining to focus on the light clouds, lest his life escape him should he lose sight of them. He could feel the warmth of his blood pooling beneath him. His mind conjured up an unsolicited image of the fabric of his mother's apron, a blue-floral print that was so familiar to him as a child when he would hug her after coming in from his chores. He could smell her bodily scent as if she were standing by his side. His last thought was of Rebecca, her image appearing before his eyes. Then all went blank.

Chapter 34

The people of Granville were eager to hear of the events surrounding Washington's march south. Almost daily, Jacob, Hut and Jon Bear trekked to the White Horse Tavern to hear the news, which traveled swiftly up and down the east coast by horse courier. Placards were posted almost every other day with news of the war that was as recent as one week old.

From time to time, Rebecca, Mehti and Sarah would join the men to get firsthand news and forego the wait of the men's return from the White Horse. Even old man Cuthbert would join the group as they made their way across the town green to the news board outside the building, where such bulletins were posted. Every evening around dinner time, people gathered to read the latest news postings.

In early October, a posting dated September 19, 1781 read, "Washington's Continentals and Rochambeau arrive at Williamsburg, Join Marquis de Lafayette." A few weeks later another posting relayed that "Joint Armies March to Yorktown, British Surrounded."

"What does it say about the Hussars?" Rebecca kept asking.

"Nothing is being said in today's bulletin," Jacob responded every time she asked.

Then in mid-October, word of the Hussars finally made its way to Granville. The tavern keeper read the bulletin out loud as several of the townspeople listened.

"On October third, Claude Gabriel de Choisy, with the support of Brigadier General George Weeden's Virginia militia and the French Legions and Hussars under the command of Duc de Lauzun, were victorious in battle against British troops under the command of Lieutenant Colonel Thomas Dundas and Lieutenant Colonel Banastre Tarleton, and supported by the Twenty-Third Royal Welsh Fusiliers on the plains at Gloucester Point, Virginia. At the conclusion of the encounter, the embattled British retreated to their redoubts, where they are being kept at bay as the war rages on in Yorktown across the York River. British casualties are said to number thirteen. The French suffered three killed and sixteen wounded, while the Americans suffered two killed and eleven wounded. Lieutenant Colonel Banastre Tarleton was among the British wounded."

"Do they name the French killed or wounded?" Rebecca asked immediately.

"No names here, Rebecca," the tavern keeper replied.

"Rebecca," Jacob said as he put a hand on her shoulder. "There were most likely two or three thousand soldiers fighting for us at Gloucester. What is the likelihood that Frederic has been killed or wounded? It's highly unlikely I would say."

"The odds of his return are likely," Rebecca said, "but I would so like an assurance."

"Then I assure you, dear sister, Frederic will return to you. There, does that make you feel better?" he said with squeeze of her shoulder.

"You do yourself no good if you wallow in negative thoughts," Mehti told her sister.

Over the next few weeks, Rebecca checked the mail every other day, looking for some word from Frederic. But nothing came. News of the assault on Yorktown continued to be posted. The town had been bombarded continuously by the Americans and French. French Admiral De Grasse's fleet had intercepted and outnumbered the British fleet at the mouth of the York River. Then on October 26th came the most incredible news of all.

BE IT REMEMBERED!

That on the 17th day of October, 1781,

Lieut. Gen. Charles Earl Cornwallis, with

Above 5,000 British troops,

Surrendered themselves prisoners of war

To his Excellency Gen. George Washington,

Commander in chief of the combined allied forces

Of America and France.

LAUS DEO!

And then this bulletin:

YORKTOWN IS WON!

CORNWALLIS' SWORD DELIVERED TO AMERICAN FORCES.

"The World Turned Upside Down"

And another, two days later:

IMPORTANT INTELLIGENCE:

NEWPORT, October 25th, 1781

YESTERDAY afternoon arrived in this harbor, Captain LOVETT, of the Schooner Adventure, from York River, in Chesapeake Bay, which it left the 20th instance and brought us the GLORIOUS NEWS of the SURRENDER of LORD CORNWALLIS and his ARMY. Prisoners of War to the Allied army under the command of our illustrious General and the French fleet, under the command of his Excellency the Count De Grasse.

A cessation of arms took place on Thursday, the 18th instant. In consequence of proposals from Lord CORNWALLIS for a capitulation—His Lordship proposed a cessation of TWENTY-FOUR HOURS—but TWO ONLY were granted by his Excellence General WASHINGTON. The articles were completed the same day, and the next day the Allied army took possession of YORKTOWN.

By this Glorious conquest NINE THOUSAND of the Enemy, including Seamen, fell into our hands, with an immense quantity of warlike stores and forty Gun Ships, a Frigate and Armed Vessel and about ONE HUNDRED SAIL of TRANSPORTS.

But the bulletin that most caught Rebecca's eye a week later provided the following:

The Battle of Yorktown

The Numbers

Troops:

British	9,700
American & French	17,000

Ships:

French Fleet – 24 Ships

British Fleet – 19 Ships

Casualties (approximate):

American – 20 dead, 56 wounded

French -   52 dead, 134 wounded

British -   600 dead & wounded

The people of Granville were jubilant. The church bell rang out and the White Horse Tavern was a central location for celebration. Virtually all conversation centered on what would happen next. There were currently approximately 10,000 British troops positioned in New York. Would they be asked to leave? What would happen to the thousands of British prisoners taken at Yorktown? In spite of the many unanswered questions, gaiety prevailed. And Rebecca had only one question—what had become of Frederic? If he were killed or wounded, how could she find out? Frederic's only friend who had known of her had been executed by firing squad. Dare she write to the Duc de Lauzun and ask of Frederic's situation? There was no peace of mind for her until she could know for sure what had become of him. As the days wore on with no word from him, Rebecca felt less and less certain that Jacob's prediction of Frederic's return would come to pass.

Chapter 35

The tent's heat was stifling. Temperatures had been unusually high for early November, even for Williamsburg.

"Doctor!" Frederic's tent mate, Armand, called out. The doctor had been tending to wounded from both the battle at Yorktown and the battle at Gloucester Point. Most of the men had been transported to the hospital at Williamsburg, but capacity had been reached and tents were set up in a nearby field to manage the overflow of patients.

The doctor came rushing into the tent.

"You told me to call you if I saw any sign at all. His eyelids began fluttering. That's a good sign, correct?" the soldier said.

"Let me take a look," the doctor said, bending over Frederic's cot. He felt his head for signs his fever had broken.

"His fever has gone down, so there is hope," the doctor said. "I'll have the boy bring fresh well water. Continue with the compresses." The doctor lifted the bandages that covered Frederic's right torso and examined the wound that displayed the point of bullet entry, as well as the unavoidable tissue damage brought about by the bullet's removal. "He's a very lucky man," the doctor said as he eyed the wound. "I see signs the swelling have abated and the wound may be healing. It certainly is no worse, so that's a good sign. I won't need to bleed him again. You need to let some air into this tent."

"The gnats are plaguing us and I wanted to keep him as comfortable as possible," Armand replied.

"Have the boy bring some netting. Some arrived just yesterday," the doctor said as he patted Armand on the shoulder. "It looks like our Captain Dubois is going to live."

Finally, Frederic opened his eyes and looked up at Armand, who immediately lifted Frederic's head and gave him a sip of water. Frederic gagged as he drank.

"Easy, Frederic." Armand rested his friend's head back onto his bedroll.

"What happened? Where am I?" Frederic asked.

"You're at a hospital outpost in Williamsburg. We brought you here after you were wounded at Gloucester Point. Good news, Frederic: The British have surrendered at Yorktown. The war is over!" Armand exclaimed.

"What happened at Gloucester?"

"I saw you fall from your horse, but I could not get to you. I thought you were dead for certain, but when the British were pushed back to their redoubts, you were examined and found to be alive, but unconscious. We brought you here and the bullet was removed successfully. The doctor said time would tell whether or not you would regain consciousness. I am pleased to say you are holding up well.

"While the battle at Yorktown raged on for many days with bombardments that were deafening even on our side of the river, we held siege to the British holed up on Gloucester Point—who dared not leave their strongholds. Perhaps they thought Cornwallis would come to their rescue. But Cornwallis will be rescuing no one," Armand said with a laugh. "And Tarleton was wounded. How magnificent, I ask you? The day after the surrender, General Washington invited all the officers—American, French and British—to dine with him. All except Tarleton. I would say he received Washington's message of dismissal quite plainly."

"They all dined together?" Frederic said in a whisper of disbelief.

"Here, take another sip of water."

"And what of our unit?"

"The Duc de Lauzun has already disembarked for France. He left within two days of the surrender. Our orders are to stay in Virginia for now. And you, my friend, must focus all your attention and strength on getting well," Armand said.

"I must write to Rebecca."

"You must rest. I will write to her on your behalf, but now you must rest."

Frederic reached up and grabbed Armand's tunic sleeve as he started to get up from his stool. "Armand, I must return to France. When I was wounded, I saw an image of my mother as clearly as if she was standing next to me," he said, straining to muster the energy to complete his sentence. "It was a clear message to me, or at least it raises in me a desire to return home."

"As you wish, Frederic. I can write the letter for you tomorrow, I promise. But for right now, do not upset yourself. You need to rest, my friend."

Frederic's arm dropped limply to the cot, his energy spent, and he immediately fell to sleep.

Two days later, on Armand's regular visit to Frederic's tent, he found his friend propped up on his cot, a bowl of porridge resting on his chest. He was slowly and painstakingly feeding himself. He looked up at Armand, a smile consuming his expression.

"You are strengthened!" Armand said with delight.

"Yes. It appears I will live." Frederic joked. Then his tone turned serious. "Armand, I need you to write to Rebecca for me. My hands are not steady," he said holding his left hand in the air and watching it tremble.

"I will get a quill, paper and ink. Perhaps a board to write on if I can find one."

Armand returned after a short time and sat upon a barrel, his ink pot nearby, a board and paper in his lap.

"How shall I begin?" he asked Frederic.

Frederic began to dictate his letter.

November 8, 1781

My Dearest Rebecca,

I am so grateful to be able to dictate this letter to you with the help of my friend, Armand, whom I take into my complete confidence.

What great joy that the war is over and that we have been victorious! But in battle I have sustained an injury for which I require time to recover. I am laid low at a hospital in Williamsburg and will remain here until I am well enough to endure travel.

Today I write to tell you that my injury and close encounter with my own demise has given me pause and a need to return to my homeland. My heart beckons from a call across the Atlantic that I cannot ignore. It had been my intent to return to you and to Granville, but inexplicably, I cannot deny my need to return home.

Please forgive me. I know not what the future holds, and would not ask that you wait for me. But I will write if I may. I anticipate that I will return to France as soon as I am able. Know that I will think of you daily as long as I breathe.

All my love to you,

Frederic

"Are you quite certain of this?" Armand asked. "What you're doing makes little sense to me, and I feel it may also make no sense to your lady friend."

"I don't expect you to understand, Armand. I barely understand it myself," Frederic replied.

Chapter 36

The mid-November winds were beginning their boisterous torrent across the green of Granville and leaves swirled around the feet of Mehti and Rebecca as they swung Oliver by the arms between them. He chortled in glee with every air lift.

The sisters headed toward White Horse Tavern—Mehti for the latest news, Rebecca for word from Frederic. The harvest was all in, and wood had been stacked for the winter months. They could sense the winding down of life, especially with the conclusion of the war. The crisp fall air was filled with the aroma of falling leaves. With their free hands, the women clasped their shawls around their necks and leaned into the wind.

The folks in Granville celebrated heartily after the surrender at Yorktown. Rum flowed more freely than it ought, and men built bonfires on the green several nights in a row. A barn dance added to the festivities; the women whose husbands had yet to return danced with each other.

While the White family was relieved the war was over, there were still some questions about the formal ending of the war, and in particular what would become of the 10,000 British troops occupying the city of New York? And what of this new country? Would each state govern itself? Would the colonies combine under one government and, if so, who would run that government? These questions consumed the minds of the townspeople, and fed the discourse around the tables at the White Horse.

Rebecca entered the tavern and headed directly for the bar, as she had done several times a week since the surrender, to ask whether any mail had arrived. Each time the tavern keeper had given her the same answer—"No Rebecca, nothing today."

But on this day, when she asked if there were a letter for her, the tavern keeper responded with a big smile. "Yes, Rebecca, there is a letter for you," and he handed her the sealed piece of parchment.

Rebecca stared at the letter blankly, then looked up at Mehti.

"What is it, Rebecca?"

"This is not Frederic's handwriting. I know his handwriting and this is not his," Rebecca said, a wave of concern sweeping across her anguished face. "I fear what this means, Mehti. Why would someone else be writing to me, except to tell me Frederic has perished?" Her eyes began to well up with tears. Her hands began to tremble. She handed the letter to Mehti. "I cannot read this. Mehti, please read it for me."

The two women found seats at a nearby table, the tavern being mostly empty at that time of day. Rebecca hoisted Oliver onto her lap and Mehti unfolded the letter.

She read through it quickly, then looked up at her sister. "He lives and is only wounded," Mehti told her.

Rebecca gasped with relief, her hand to her mouth, lest she cry out. "How serious are his injuries? Does it say?"

"No, it just says he's been wounded and is in Williamsburg recuperating."

"Thank God, Mehti!" Rebecca exclaimed. "My worst fears have been put to rest."

"There's more," Mehti said, her voice barely a whisper. She handed the letter to Rebecca and took Oliver onto her lap.

Rebecca read Frederic's letter in disbelief. "What cruel twist is this?" Rebecca stammered to her sister. "I feel I cannot believe what I am reading. I must write him immediately. This wrong must be put to right. I am elated that he is alive, but to never see him again?" She began to cry softly, which in turn caused Oliver to begin crying. "Forgive me, my son," Rebecca said to Oliver, kissing his forehead. "I must count my blessings that I have you in my life," she said, taking her son back onto her lap and hugging him fiercely.

"It is a peculiar outcome, Becca, but I am happy that you know he is alive," Mehti said.

Rebecca looked into her sister's eyes, and there she saw the loss her sister still felt from Caleb's death at sea. "What is to become of us, Mehti? We are not unlike two war widows suffering their losses. I feel I am grieving so," she said as the two of them began to make their way back across the green toward home, in slow, reluctant steps.

Halfway across the green, Rebecca paused. "I mustn't feel sorry for myself, Mehti. Look at what has happened to the people of New London and the surrounding towns. So many real widows, so many fatherless children, so many people without a hearth or a scrap of food going into the winter. My heart breaks for the Perkins family the most—losing six members of their family in one day. And Mrs. Ledyard losing her husband and her with an infant child. No, Mehti, I need to talk with the Reverend and pray for the gratitude it is evident I am lacking."

"And we must never forget their sacrifice, dear sister," Mehti added.

Then the two women continued on to the warmth of their home.

Chapter 37

Spring - 1782

In truth, the war dragged on. But what was also true was that neither the British nor the colonists had the stomach to continue. Major General of the Continental Army, Nathanael Greene and his troops monitored South Carolina while the British lingered in Charleston. Greene's attempts to recruit additional men from Virginia, Maryland and Delaware bore little response. Soldiers had not been paid, and unless monies could be raised, chances of attracting fighters to continue the cause, if needed, were slim.

Shortly after the British surrender at Yorktown, the Comte de Grasse and his French fleet sailed for the West Indies to continue to engage the British fleet that had moved into Caribbean waters. By December, Lafayette had returned to France in time to celebrate the birth of the first child of Louis XVI and Marie Antoinette.

General Washington and his army marched north to Newburgh, New York, to keep a watch on the British troops that lingered in New York. Also in December, the traitor, Benedict Arnold, requested a leave of absence from the British Army to return to London with his wife. Britain to date had not offered up a peace agreement. The Hussars remained in Virginia awaiting further orders. Such was the news that had reached the townspeople of Granville.

In New London, the people had barely began to rebuild their town, so poor and tired from the events of the previous September. Charred ship remains poked their heads out of the bays of the Thames River. Debris from burned buildings still littered the town, lone chimneys standing like sentinels, testaments and constant reminders of the cruelty of the British. But spring brought warm weather and a sense of renewal, in spite of the pain of loss and mourning that had gripped the town over the winter months. Townsfolk could grow produce to feed their families. Many applied to the General Assembly for assistance and compensation for loss. Life would move on.

Mehti bent over her hoe, turning over the soil in the kitchen garden, while Ruthie Cuthbert sat on a nearby bench and listened to the birds render their spring mating songs. A new wagon had been built and, as soon as drier days were upon them and the roads were groomed and passable, Hut, Jacob and old man Cuthbert planned to start weekly treks to New London to remove burned debris of the store and butcher shop. Then they would haul loads of seasoned wood south with plans for a rudimentary, livable building to be completed before the fall. The only salvageable thing that remained of the building was the hearth stone.

"Well, we can start with that," old man Cuthbert had said, ever so pragmatic.

The gnats buzzed around Mehti's bonnet in the early-morning hour, and she had to swat them away at least once for every time her hoe gouged the earth. Finally, in frustration, she rested both hands on the handle and considered quitting the task until later in the day. When she looked up, a strange man stood perfectly still at the end of their yard, staring at her. His shoulders were broad, displaying a sign of strength and youth, but his clothes were those of a vagrant and his hair was not properly tied. His light-colored beard was long, bushy and also ungroomed. A rucksack was strung over one shoulder and he gently removed it and placed it on the ground next to him, as though he intended to stay. She wondered what he wanted and why he stood so perfectly still and silent.

"Mehti?" the man said.

She was taken aback, for surely she did not know this strange man. His voice was deep and unfamiliar to her.

"Mehti, it's me, Caleb."

A jolt of disbelief consumed Mehti, leaving her motionless and without words.

"Truly, Mehti, it is me," Caleb insisted.

"Mehti, what is it?" Ruthie called from her bench.

Mehti dropped her hoe and stepped slowly toward Caleb, still in disbelief. "Caleb? Caleb Rogers? *My* Caleb Rogers?"

"Well, I like the sound of that," Caleb said jokingly, hoping to remove some of the shock his arrival undoubtedly had caused. He had dreamt of this moment for over a year and now that it had finally come, he could think of nothing more endearing to say.

Mehti lifted her skirts and made her way across the garden, talking as she went. "I thought you drowned, Caleb! All this time, I thought you drowned! My God, man!" she yelled as she made her way to him. Reaching him, she looked into his familiar brown eyes, affirmation to her heart.

"Mehti, what is it?" Ruthie called out again.

"Hush a moment, Ruthie. All is well," Mehti called back to Ruthie as her eyes remained locked on Caleb's, afraid he might disappear if she were to look away. She reached out and touched him, to be sure he wasn't an apparition.

He drew her to himself and took her into his arms. "I am real, Mehti," he whispered into her ear. Mehti melted into him like raindrops on moss.

"I can't believe it," she said. Then her eyes popped open and an unexpected fury took hold of her. She pushed herself away and began pounding on his chest. "Caleb Rogers, how could you do this to me? How could you be gone so long without a word! I thought you dead this last year! Where have you been?"

Caleb grabbed her wrists to stop her torrent. "Mehti, I had been hijacked on a boat out of Long Island. I've been sailing on a trading vessel throughout the Caribbean, the Atlantic, the Mediterranean, determined to work my way back home—back home to you."

Mehti released herself from his grip and began pacing back and forth in front of him in a rant. "Don't you act as though you care for me! If you cared for me at all, you would have written in every port you entered."

"I was not allowed off ship, for fear I would escape."

Mehti huffed and stood facing him, her arms across her chest. "I've been in mourning all this time, Caleb. I thought you were dead." She began to cry, and he took her into his arms again.

"Forgive me, Mehti. If you can't forgive me, then I would wish to die."

Mehti stood back again, wiped her eyes and studied him more closely. "Well, you certainly have grown to be a man."

"Life at sea will do that to a boy. But I am seventeen now, Mehti, and I've experienced much and seen so many different places, if even from the ship. The only time I was allowed to go on shore was in Barcelona, with the captain and the first mate. The world is so different from Granville. But I was never able to get word to you. Believe me, I tried." Caleb reached into his rucksack and pulled out a stack of letters. "These are for you," he said, handing her the letters. "I wrote whenever I could find paper, pen and ink."

Mehti turned the letters over in her hand and felt her anger melting away.

"I have so much to tell you, Mehti. But first I must ask, have there been any comers for you since I left?"

"Comers?" She shook her head, trying to understand what he was asking. Then it occurred to her. "No, Caleb—there have been no comers. I have been in mourning."

"Then I must see your father," Caleb said, his voice suddenly full of urgency. "All I have thought about for this last year is this moment, to return to you and hope we can make a life together. I've saved every pence I earned, and I will waste no time on this, Mehti."

"Shush," Mehti said covering his mouth with her hand to silence him. "Father passed in the fall—an accident with a sickle while working the fields."

"I am so sorry, Mehti." Caleb paused for only a moment. "Then it is Jacob I seek." They leaned into each other, forehead to forehead.

"This is all too much for me to absorb, Caleb," Mehti said, shaking her head. "I need some time."

"I will give you all the time you need, Mehti. But I will not let you go."

Finally, Mehti took Caleb by the hand. "Come, I want you to meet Ruthie. I have much to tell you as well, Caleb."

Epilogue

December 1, 1781

My Dearest Frederic –

I hope you are well and recovering from your wounds.

I have been a woman of both joy and misery since receiving your letter. I feel utter joy that you have survived the battle at Gloucester, so consumed was I with fear of what might have befallen you. Hopefully your injuries will heal quickly and the doctors will hasten your recovery.

My sadness comes at the thought of never seeing you again. A reunion had been so prominent in my mind in hope you would survive the trials of the war. Knowing you will not be returning to Granville has been hard for me to grasp. I have been in consult with Reverend Miller and he has helped me see I must not burden you with my sadness. Simply put, I must understand your need to return home, and I shall do so.

Will you write to me, Frederic? You have said you will keep me in your thoughts daily, and you shall be in mine, dearest. Please do write to me.

Yours affectionately,

Rebecca

January 12, 1782

My Sweet Rebecca,

What manner of man is this, I ask you, who hobbles about the encampment, low of energy and stamina? If I endeavor to consider of what value I would be to anyone in this state of physical disrepair, I cringe to think myself worthy of anyone's company. I applaud my friend, Armand, who helps to keep my mind active with conversation and games. We, all of us, have too much time on our hands.

I had thought to be boarded on a ship out of Charleston, but as long as I am improving, I am stationed to remain here with the legion. There is talk of us moving to Wilmington later in the year and that is as much as I know. I still feel this strong need to return to France to see my mother once again. We have exchanged letters and she is eager for my return as well.

Of course I will write to you, my sweet Rebecca. My memories are so fond and sustain me, how could I not?

With Love and affection,

Frederic

February 1, 1782

Dearest Frederic,

Our winter has been particularly brutal. Jon Bear and Sarah keep to their barn cabin as do Hut, Ruby and Malcolm—the snow is so deep we rarely venture out. On Sundays, we all attend church and have our one meal of the week together in the afternoon. How fortunate for you that you live in more temperate climes.

In the evenings, after dinner and once the children are down, Mehti, Ruthie, Rachael and I sit near the fire and do our needlework. Jacob and Robert Cuthbert relax on the fringes, talking of town concerns while smoking their pipes. Rachael has grown so large from her pregnancy that she scarcely has a lap upon which to set her handiwork. She is able to rest it on top of her stomach and thereby keep her stitches close. The doctor says she could deliver any day now. In this wintry weather, the doctor will not be summoned and Sarah will midwife.

I write of these events and scenes to keep you apprised of our life in Granville, since you cannot be here. Perhaps one day you will be able to return and it will be as though you never left. I enclose a lock of my hair so that you might remember me often.

I have heard that John Adams and his wife, Abigail, have been apart more in their marriage than they have been together, due to his diplomatic responsibilities. They continue their loving relationship through their correspondence. My fondest desire is that we are able to do so as well.

Please write to me soon.

> *With all my affection,*
>
> *Rebecca*

February 24, 1782

Dear Rebecca,

What a pleasure it has been for me to finally be well enough to ride, although the doctor has given me strict orders to only walk my horse as anything more would jostle my body and usurp the internal healing that has taken place. How pleased I was to discover that my doctor also serves the medical needs of George Washington when he is in Virginia. I feel optimistic I have been in the best of medical hands.

You are correct, my dearest, that the weather here has been quite mild. In their boredom, the men have been exploring the outskirts at safe distances, grooming their horses, strolling the town in the evenings and visiting the taverns. A curfew keeps them straight, lest they spend too much time imbibing.

I thank you for the news of your family and I do feel as if I am there, as I can picture it very well. I can imagine you sitting by the fire—the flames aglow in your eyes, your smile brightening the room. And I remember our one kiss as *though it happened yesterday. Indeed, I believe relationships can carry on through this venue.*

Love and affection,

Frederic

One week after receiving Frederic's most recent letter, Jacob picked up another letter at the tavern addressed to Rebecca. He handed her the letter that evening after dinner. The handwriting was not Frederic's, and Rebecca was again overcome with fear for his safety. She gazed at the seal on the letter—the discernable "**A**" stamped in red wax indicated the letter was from Armand.

Her family watched her carefully open the letter, her hands trembling. She read it aloud.

March 1, 1782

Dear Mrs. Tewkesbury:

I write at the request of, and on behalf of, Frederic Dubois, who is indisposed. Frederic received word just yesterday that his mother, Amelina Dubois, died in Alsace, France, due to consumption. As you are aware, it was his wish to return to France and see his mother, prompted by her vision that appeared to him at the time he sustained his injury on the battlefield. The news of her death has caused him considerable distress and I write to you so you are apprised these events. If I may be of any further service to you, please write in response.

Sincerely,

Armand

Rebecca sat wide-eyed in disbelief. Again, her feelings were mixed—a sadness for Frederic that he was not able to fulfill his wish to see his mother, but also an optimism that now he could return to her—to Granville. She looked to Jacob. "What shall I do, Jacob?"

"A letter of condolence is certainly in order," Jacob said as he filled his pipe and tamped it down. "I would say nothing more, Becca. I believe it would be unwise to put undue pressure on the man. He must come to Granville of his own accord. Consider, if you will, what a former French soldier would do in this country? Do you expect he would become a farmer? What form of misery would that be for soldier and gentleman? Think on this Rebecca."

Rebecca looked down at the letter and slowly nodded in agreement.

"I will think on this, Jacob, and I will send my condolences tomorrow.

March 15, 1782

Dearest Frederic,

I received word this day from Armand that your mother has passed. My family and I send to you our deepest sympathies. My heart goes out to you, Frederic, and my family and I stand ready to console you in any way you feel it wanted.

With love and sympathy,

Rebecca

May 3, 1782

Dear Rebecca,

I have been grieving so, my mood so solemn. Please forgive me as I have dared not write while feeling so low.

Spring brings with it a sense of renewal, does it not? One can wallow only so long, my dearest, and I feel I am at a turning point in my life.

You may think me a romantic, but my grief has been soothed by the morning sounds of the meadowlark, by the luminous moonlight, by the waves that constantly arrive on the shore, never ending. Nature speaks the language of continued life, or at the very least, a cycle of living.

I propose to you, sweet Rebecca, that I change course in my life and resign my commission from the legion. The glories of war are rife with falsehoods and no longer appeal.

I propose to you, sweet Rebecca, that upon my release, I return to Granville, if you will have me. Please contemplate this possibility. Soldiering has been in my blood the last few years. I feel a calling I have yet to discover, but with your help, will endeavor to unearth that calling.

Please consider my proposals and return your answer as soon as you are able.

Yours with affection,

Frederic

Rebecca laid Frederic's letter in her lap. There had been so many tears in recent months, but her tears now were tears of joy. There was no doubt as to her response. How quickly life could change, could up end. Caleb's recent return had proven that to her, and now Frederic would be returning as well.

For every ending in life, there are prospects for a new beginning, Rebeca thought as she held Frederic's letter to her bosom.

Historical Context

From the Connecticut Gazette of Friday, September 7th, 1781

AN ACCOUNT

OF THE

BURNING OF NEW LONDON

ON THE

6TH OF SEPTEMBER, 1781

At about day-break on Thursday morning last, twenty-four sail of the enemy's shipping appeared to the westward of this harbor, which by many were supposed to be a plundering party after stock.

Alarm guns were immediately fired, but the discharge of cannon in the harbor has become so frequent of late that they answered little or no purpose. The defenceless state of the fortifications and town are obvious to our readers. A few of the inhabitants who were equipped advanced toward the place where the enemy were tho't likely to make their landing, and maneuvered on the heights adjacent, until the enemy, about 9 o'clk, landed in two divisions of about 800 men each, one of them at Brown's farm near the lighthouse, the other at Groton point. The division that landed near the light-house marched up the road, keeping out large flanking parties, who were attacked in different places on their march by the inhabitants who had spirit and resolution to oppose their progress; the main body of the enemy proceeded to the town and set fire to the stores on the beach, and immediately after to the dwelling-houses lying on the Mill Cove. The scattered fire of our little parties unsupported by our neighbours more distant galled them, so that they soon began to retire, setting fire to stores and dwelling-houses promiscuously in their way; the fire from the stores communicated to the shipping that lay at the wharfs, and a number were burnt; others swung to single fasts and remained unburnt. At 4o'clk they began to quit the town with great precipitation, and were pursued by our brave citizens in the spirit of veterans and drove on board their boats. Five of the enemy were killed and about 20 wounded. Among the latter is a Hessian captain who is a prisoner, as are seven others. We lost four killed and ten or twelve wounded—none mortal. The most valuable part of the town is reduced to ashes, and all the stores. Fort Trumbull not being tenable on the land side, was evacuated as the enemy advanced, and the few men in it crossed the river to Fort Griswold, on Groton Hill, which was soon after invested by the division that landed on the point. The fort having in it only 120 men, chiefly militia, hastily collected who defended it with the greatest resolution and bravery, and once repulsed the enemy, but the fort being out of repair could not be defended by such a handful of men, th° brave and determined, against so superior a number, they did ALL that men of spirit and bravery in such a situation could do; but after having a number of their party killed and wounded they found that further resistance would be in vain, and resigned the fort. Immediately on their surrender the valient Colonel Ledyard, whose fate in a particular manner is much lamented, and 70 other officers and men, were murdered, most of them heads of families. The enemy lost a Major Montgomery and forty-one officers and men in the attack, who were found near the fort; their wounded were carried off. Soon after the enemy got possession of the fort they set fire to and burnt a number of dwelling-houses and stores on Groton bank, and embarked about sunset, taking with them sundry of the inhabitants of New London and Groton. A Colonel Ayres, who commanded the division, was wounded, and it is said died on board the fleet the night they embarked.

About 15 sail of vessels with effects of the inhabitants retreated up the river on the approach of the enemy, and were saved, and four others remained in the harbor unhurt. The troops were commanded by that infamous traitor to his country, Benedict Arnold, who headed the division which proceeded to the town. By this calamity it is judged that more than one hundred families are deprived of their habitations, and most of their ALL. This neighborhood feel sensibly the loss of many deserving citizens, and, th⁰ deceased canˢᵗ but be highly indebted to them for their spirit and bravery in their exertions and manly opposition to the merciless enemies of our country in their last moments.

<u>Note to Reader</u>: This novel takes place in the fictitious town of Granville, Connecticut, where I place the Hussar encampment in the winter of 1780 and 1781. I took liberties. In fact, the Hussars encamped in the town of Lebanon, Connecticut, for that time period. Another fact is they did not camp on the town green, a veritable swamp at the time, but rather west of the green, on land owned by Governor Jonathan Trumbull. When I envision the town of Granville, it appears in my imagination as the lovely town of Lebanon.

The End...for now.

Recommended Reading

Allyn, Charles. *Battle of Groton Heights: A Collection of Narratives, Official Reports, Records, Etc. of the Storming of Fort Griswold.* Connecticut, 1882.

Di Bonaventura, Allegra. *For Adam's Sake: A Family Saga in Colonial New England.* New York: W.W. Norton and Company, Inc., 2013.

Ferling, John. *Whirlwind: The American Revolution and the War that Won It.* New York, London, New Dehli and Sydney: Bloomsbury Press, 2015.

Ketchum, Richard M. *Victory at Yorktown: The Campaign that Won the Revolution.* New York: Henry Holt and Company, 2004.

Lehman, Eric D. *Homegrown Terror: Benedict Arnold and the Burning of New London.* Middletown, Connecticut: Wesleyan University Press, 2014.

Philbrick, Nathaniel. *Valient Ambition: George Washington, Benedict Arnold and the Fate of the American Revolution.* New York: Penguin Books, 2017.

Martin, David Plum. *A Narrative of a Revolutionary War Soldier.* New York: American Library, 2001.

Selig, Robert. *March to Victory: Washington, Rochambeau, and the Yorktown Campaign of 1781.* University of Michigan Digital Library. HP Publishing reprint, 2017.

Selig, Robert. *Hussars in Lebanon! A Connecticut Town and Lauzun's Legion During the American Revolution.* Connecticut: Lebanon Historical Society Publication, 2004.

<u>Connect with me on line</u>:

If you enjoyed reading my novel, please feel free to provide me with feedback.

E-mail: jogillespie@aol.com

Website: www.jogillespie.com

Facebook: www.facebook.com/JoGillespie

www.ingramcontent.com/pod-product-compliance
Lightning Source LLC
Chambersburg PA
CBHW020601180626
46810CB00007B/2597